Ty doesn't say anything, but he reaches out and brushes my hair back with his rings, all twelve of them, glittering and sparkling like rubies. They match the piercings in his face. Gotta love a color coordinated badass.

Neither of us misses how small and tight this bathroom is, how close we are, how hard he was in the kitchen.

"Ty," I warn as he comes up behind me and slides his fingers under my shirt, up my belly, cupping my tender breasts with strong hands. "So not fair," I groan, reaching up and smacking the fan. It coughs to life and is loud as fuck, blocking any sounds from escaping this little room. "You can't touch those." My cunt is pulsing and my heart is pounding in my skull. Down below, I know I'm soaking wet.

"Why not?" he whispers against my ear. "It'll make you feel better."

Books by
C.M. Stunich

Never Can Tell

Never too Late

C.M. STUNICH

SARIAN ROYAL

to the ones that Never meant to find love, but found it anyway.
congratulations.

1

Ty is going to die.

I chew my nails as I watch him moving across the roof of the house. *Our house. Your house. This belongs to you.* I shake my head and look away, partially because I really am terrified that Ty is going to fall off and break his neck and partially because that statement doesn't just apply to the house. It also applies to the baby I've got strapped to my damn chest. Ty drew pictures of bullets in Sharpie over the straps of the carrier to make me feel better about wearing the fucking thing, but I still feel like a tool. Not even fake ammo belts can make me change my mind about that. *This belongs to you,* too, I repeat, but the words feel even less real than the ones that pertain to this shambling lemon of ours.

"Ty!" I call, and my heart plunges to the floor of my stomach when he trips on a loose shingle and has to grab onto the chimney to stay upright. "Fuck," I snarl as I lift my hands to my head. I can't take the nerves right now. I just fucking can't. "Tyson McCabe, get your ass off the goddamn roof!" He looks down at me and grins which makes things all the worse because even as I'm worrying about his safety, I'm checking out his chest. Sweat glistens on the sharply defined muscles there, promising me that despite Ty's new status as *daddy*, he's still hot as shit. I swallow hard.

"As soon as I figure out where the leak is coming from, I'm all yours, baby," he tells me as he scoots forward and drops to his knees, crawling across the roof like an inked up god, bracelets jingling in the still, gray air. The man is infuriating as shit. Water starts to drip into the nursery and within hours, he's trying to commit suicide by scrambling across the wet roof. Can't even fucking wait until the rain stops.

Droplets smack my skull and make me even more irritated; they make Noah cry. He starts softly at first, but then breaks down into these ear piercing wails that I know come from McCabe's half of the genealogy; I was a quiet baby. I bounce up and down, again feeling sort of stupid doing it, and have to shove a cigarette between my lips like a damn pacifier. I can't smoke it when Noah's around, but even the feeling of my mouth clamped down around makes me calmer, like I can absorb the tobacco through my saliva. Maybe I should start chewing?

With a regretful sigh, I move onto the porch and push Chuck Norris out of the way with my foot. The stupid cat refuses to come inside unless Ty's in the house. I think this dumb as fuck tabby could use some therapy or counseling or something. Clearly, he has an obsession.

I move across the scratched up floors and into the kitchen where a microwave, a portable cooktop, and a mini fridge remain the only appliances. It's kind of tough shit when you need to buy something and don't have any money. *Other than your husband's leftover stores of fuck money that is.* I look down at baby Noah and try to rationalize putting my tit in his mouth. Don't get me wrong, and please don't think I'm a terrible mother, but I kind of, sort of hate it. I decide on a bottle and try to get it ready before Ty comes in and sees. He really hates it when I use formula. I rationalized with him by asking if he, himself, would like to put his nipple in his son's mouth. When the answer was no, he really wouldn't like to do that, we moved on. But don't think I don't see the looks he gives me when I crack out the bottle.

Unfortunately, he makes it inside right as I'm slipping the rubber nipple over the plastic.

"Oh, huh," he says when he sees this, standing there dripping wet and covered in bright red scrapes and bruises. I slam the top onto the bottle and screw it into place, glaring at him, daring him to say something. He says nothing. "Think I figured out where the fucking leak is," he tells me. Noah, who had previously quieted down, begins to scream again.

Ty doesn't hesitate in moving forward and helping me get him out of the carrier. He even slips off his shirt and dries off with a dish towel before reaching out and taking his son in his beautiful, inked up arms, bracelets sliding down his wrist as he feeds him the bottle.

"You have no fucking clue how sexy you look," I tell him as I scoot past and light my cigarette, moving towards the front door and stepping outside, so I can look in at Ty and

Noah from the porch. I make sure that the smoke drifts away from the screen and out towards the orange and yellow leaves that litter our front yard. He just grins at me and his dimples show.

"You want to show me how sexy you think I am?"

I pull my cigarette out with two fingers and give him a raised eyebrow.

"Maybe after you put your son down," I say to which his grin smolders into a smirk, burning the hair of my eyebrows and singing my eyelashes. I look away. "You're supposed to get less attractive after you have a kid," I say, dropping my cig to the deck and smashing it with my heel.

"Says who?" asks Ty as Noah finishes his bottle and starts to coo. Ty tosses it over his shoulder and actually manages to get it to land in the sink. And at an angle, too. Impressive. I shrug and start in on a second Marlboro. I kid you not, the day Noah popped out was the day I started to smoke again. And I can't seem to stop. I really should quit for good, but I don't know if I'm cut out for it. There were days there in that horrible nine month stretch where I just sat and cried and held onto my cigarettes for dear life. It's not easy to quit, no matter what anybody says.

"Says everybody," I tell him, turning my hazel eyes up to his brown ones, catching him in a breathless moment where time stands still and our black souls twine together like the dead branches on the trees in our backyard. Time slows, lets us connect, and then speeds back up again. Noah starts to cry, but Ty lifts him up and props him against one, strong, muscular shoulder, patting his back with his ringed hand and swirling his fingers around in gentle circles. "And they also say that I'm not supposed to be horny yet. Why, Ty, why is it that I'm always fucking horny?"

Ty laughs at me, and it turns into a snort as he shakes his

head and bounces up and down with our baby, not ashamed or embarrassed in the least. Ty is a much better parent than I am.

"Because I'm a fox, baby." I take a drag on my cigarette.

"You're a whore."

"I was."

"Screw you."

"Nuh, uh uh," Ty says, spinning in a slow circle, letting me see Noah's pale face and the swath of dark hair on his forehead. "If you enjoy doing it so much, you can't use it as an insult." I blow smoke out and wish I was blowing it into his face. He's infuriating sometimes, you know?

"Grow up," I tell him, but I know he already has, and at as quick a pace as is humanly possible. For the last nine, ten, whatever months, we've both come a long way. We've cleaned up this house, our lives, tried to sort out our futures. We got married. We had a *baby*. When I think about my new life in wholes and stretches, I feel sick, like it's too much, like there's no way I can be doing all of this at age twenty-two. It's much easier if I think in manageable pieces. For now, we're living on a wing and a prayer. Soon, that's going to have to change. We've been honeymooning for awhile now, and the money isn't going to last. I don't know how much of it there is, and I don't ask, but I can tell by the little crease between Ty's dark brows that it isn't much.

"I think you're a champion," Ty tells me when he's done burping Noah. "Like a fucking tiger or something, fierce and wild." I look at him, and I try not to smile. He's teasing me, sure, but he's also complimenting me, and I can't let him know how much I like it. Ty thinks because I had Noah so easily that I'm like, some kind of Sex Fertility Goddess. I think I just have wide hips, so whatever. "It's not your fault you can't keep your hands off of me." I give him another look and turn around to stab out my cigarette in the ashtray we keep on the porch and never use. There are probably a dozen butts around my feet and two in this stupid tray. I promise myself I'll make more of an effort.

When I turn back around, all I can see is Ty's retreating back as he moves up the stairs, bird tats fluttering across his slick skin. An ember of heat starts to burn in my belly, and I can't stop myself from chasing after him. The stupid tabby cat darts in behind me.

"Found the leak, huh?" I ask as Ty pauses in the doorway to our son's bedroom and watches drops of icy rain splatter against the floor. He glances over his shoulder at me, mouth in a crooked smile, eyes half-lidded.

"Found and fixed are too entirely different things, Mrs. McCabe."

"It's Ross," I tell him with a sly smile, and he just laughs. That's because we work, me and him. We work and we're fucking perfect together. Ty is the only person in the world who gets me and my dark heart and the only person I'll ever let see how deep that blackness goes, how it eventually morphs into a cluster of bright as fuck stars. "Want to put him in our bed?" I ask as Ty turns around and comes to stand next to me, filling the doorway with his warmth, his love, his heat.

My head drops to his shoulder and my breath escapes slowly, like it's being drawn from inside of me by Ty's presence. He could do that, you know, suck the life out of me, leave me for dead. He could, but he never would.

"Yeah," he whispers, voice quiet, pitched low not just for the sleeping infant clutched in his arms, but also for me, too. Ty leans over and presses a kiss to my hair, all the while keeping his son's head supported with a handful of butterflies. I didn't think it was possible to love him anymore than I did before, but I think I do. Seeing him with Noah is like seeing an entirely different side of McCabe, and I fell for that, too.

The bastard. "Come with us?" I nod and turn around, threading my fingers around Ty's bicep, sliding my nails over the wings of a blue butterfly. The sound of the rain outside and the jingle of Ty's bracelets are the only noises to be heard as we move as a unit down the hallway and into the shitty as shit room we've carved out for ourselves.

The bed, along with the rest of the furniture, belongs to me, all shipped up here courtesy of Beth. It's probably the nicest room in the house.

"Tomorrow," Ty tells me as he lays Noah down in the center of the bed and climbs in after him. "I'm getting a job." Ty says this everyday, but he never has much luck. Could be because I'm selfish and hardly ever let him go. I don't tell him this, but I'm afraid to be left alone with Noah. I don't have any motherly instincts, and I don't know what to do with him. I love him. Oh God, fuck yeah, I do, but I just don't understand him. I blame all of this on Angelica and that stupid son of a bitch, Luis. I had no parents, so I don't know how to be a parent. I keep telling myself that I'll get through it, that I'll learn how, but it isn't easy.

I ignore all of this and respond with a simple, "I love you," as I climb in opposite Ty and find his ringed hand, tangling our fingers together while our breath mingles in the space above Noah's head. We kiss once, soft, no teeth, no tongue, and then we fall asleep. Life is hard, and it's not perfect, but we're together now and that's all that matters.

Why is there always something that has to come along and screw it up?

2

Despite his best intentions, Ty does not get up the next morning to go find a job. Instead, he lays pant-less and fucking sexy as hell on our bed next to Noah. My fault for not getting up with the baby last night. I watch him from my post next to the dresser and cross my arms over my chest. Everyday it seems there's a list of things that need to be done that never actually get done. Today, I decide that I'm going to take care of some of those before either of the boys wakes up.

Might as well give it a shot anyway.

When we came here in December, I didn't expect to stay. Hell, when I left my dorm room way back when, I sure as shit didn't expect to get pregnant either. I thought I was going home to make peace with my family and break this cycle of pain that I've been living day in and day out since I was freaking five years old. That after I was done, I'd go back to school and Ty would come with. I thought we'd graduate magna cum laude and have a merry fucking time.

Instead, we're living in a rambling old shack with four rooms still filled to the gills with kitsch. Water leaks into our son's bedroom like Niagara fucking Falls, and we don't even own a freezer. Plus, we have a stupid tabby cat that pisses on everything.

"Goddamn it, Chuck," I growl as I push the cat away from a pile of clothes with my foot. "Jesus Christ, can't you do that outside?" The cat yawns and pretends it didn't just urinate in the cup of my favorite bra before wondering off. I look down at the laundry, up at the ceiling and then sigh.

Before heading down the stairs, I sneak back into the bedroom and steal a Djarum Black from our dwindled package, shoving it between my lips and pausing in the living room to grab my laptop, shipped here courtesy of Lacey Setter. I take it outside and light up, pausing to glance down at the world's laziest dog. Bitch-Angelica raises her head to look at me and snorts, dropping her muzzle back to the grass and pretending like I don't even exist. She doesn't even bother to wag her tail.

"Spoiled snot," I murmur around my cig, raising the lighter up and taking a massive drag, dropping my head back so that my hair hangs down and kisses my shoulder blades. I dyed it black again, had to. I couldn't stand waiting for the copper to grow back in, and frankly, the black sort of just suits me.

Today, I have an orange streak in the front. Could be blue next week, could be purple. I haven't been able to decide on a color lately. Like the changing leaves, my mood has been up and down and all over the fucking place. I wonder if there's something wrong with me, postpartum depression or whatever.

I exhale and scoot over to one of the plastic chairs that Ty's mother bequeathed to him along with the house. I sit in it with a huff and flip open the top to my computer. I have got to figure out how to get back in school, and take Ty with me. He keeps saying he's going to get a job, but I don't know how good of an idea that actually is. Ty might be a bad boy on the outside, but on the inside, he's a hard working man with a fierce heart. If he had to slave away at a dead end job to support Noah and me, he'd do it. I can't let that happen. Ty needs to be a therapist. He wants to help people, and I want to help him. His dream is a relatively new one, but it's a dream nonetheless. I can't let him give up the hope for something better.

I grab my cigarette in my left hand and use my right to navigate the Internet, checking my email and discovering messages from pretty much everybody I know. I scan them quickly, make sure there's no new drama that I should be aware of, and move on. I'll answer them later, if I have time. Right now, my goal is taking that next step, figuring out what Ty and I are going to do now. We have the house, the kid, the cat, the dog, now we just need the money to keep it all afloat.

I'm not out there long when I hear soft footsteps padding across the floor in the kitchen.

"Thought you could sneak a kretek without me knowing, you sneaky bitch?"

I glance over at Ty as he comes down the steps in nothing but a pair of baggy sweats. My eyes catch on his abs, the smooth slide of muscles beneath skin. I have to squeeze them shut to find my next words.

"I thought I could smoke it before you got up," I tell him as he comes over and leans down, a black cigarette dangling from his full lips. They're curved up in a deliciously infuriating smirk that makes me want to slap him and fuck him both. I light his cigarette instead, and say, "You didn't leave the baby on the bed did you?" Ty looks surprised, but not as surprised as me. Guess I have a few motherly instincts buried in there after all?

"Nah, baby, would I do something like that?" Ty smiles and winks, holding up a monitor in his ringed hand that I didn't notice before. "He's in his crib now." Ty leans down and pulls his smoke away, so he can give me a kiss. It's meant to be chaste, I think, but the hot, smoldering press of Ty's mouth against my cheek makes us both groan longingly. My hands come up automatically and trace the smooth flesh on his belly.

"It wasn't wet?" I ask him, my voice breathy and light. Ty grins and grabs the laptop, shutting the lid and tossing it onto the chair next to me. He climbs up between my legs and kneels there, leaning over me, cigarette hanging down by my ear when he puts it back in his mouth.

"No," he says as he turns the volume up on the monitor and sets it on the shelf behind my head, between an empty flower pot and a glass bottle filled with white pebbles. "But I know something that is."

Ty's hand slides up my bare thigh and under the thin, white cotton of my shirt, brushing across the fabric of my panties. Immediately, my body is no longer under my control, flaring with raging heat. My cig drops from my mouth and bounces off the arm of the chair and into the dew covered grass. My hands slide up and around Ty's neck as he pushes aside my underwear and teases my opening. I hate to fucking admit it, but I am wet. Soaked. Desperate for it. Besides, our neighbors should be used to this by now.

Ty sticks his cig into the dirt of the empty pot and drops his mouth to mine, eating me up with the taste of clover and tobacco swirling between our tongues. Ty fucks me with his fingers with one hand and pushes down his sweats with the other. Thank God, the man has enough sense not to wear any underwear. With a infant baby in the house now, it's all about speed.

McCabe teases me until I'm slick and ready, proving that he really isn't as big of a bad ass as he pretends to be. He wants to make sure I'm okay, that I can take him, that it won't hurt. And I don't think I'll ever forget that this is the same guy who kept repeating the doctor's orders: *no sex for four to six weeks.* We barely outlasted the first three and a half. Now, we're at the ten week mark and we can't keep our hands off of each other.

When he removes his hand and thrusts into me, I see stars sprinkled across the spotty sky, winking from the backs of clouds, from the bits of blue. Ty pushes up my shirt and wraps his arms around me, trailing his wet fingers across my skin. He kisses my neck, teasing my throat with the piecing in his lip as he trails molten lava over me and scalds me straight to the soul.

Wrapped up and tangled in my mussy hair, the chip earring sparkles in the sunshine like it's smiling. Neither Ty nor I pay any attention to it anymore. It's just there, has been there since I put it on and vowed never to take it off. The sex addiction seems like old news, but maybe that's only because Ty and I fuck each other so much. I don't miss the fact that that's where I go when I'm upset, the activity that I rely on when I'm stressed, but I think that's okay. When we fuck, Ty and I spin the universe into a million different shades of stark ass beauty and bloody brilliant blinding light. When our bodies meld, we conjure up the one thing this starving world needs most: true fucking love.

"You're an ass, but I love you anyway," I tell him, and I have to push back tears. I don't know why. I've been a little off lately. I thought I'd stop being so hormonal after I had the baby, but then again, I don't really know shit about kids. Guess I'm getting a firsthand education.

"I love you, too, Mrs. McCabe," he says, just to get my goat.

But it doesn't matter; Ty has my everything anyway, and I wouldn't change that for the world.

3

When Ty and I finish, we lay tangled and sweaty together on the lawn chair until bitch-Angelica comes over and starts to lick our bare feet. Ty snaps to suddenly and rises to his feet, brushing a kiss across my forehead before he heads inside and up the stairs. When he enters the room to check on Noah, I can hear him over the monitor.

"Hey there, Mini McCabe," he says, and I can't hold back a

smile, even with my panties soaked and my thighs moist, my shirt pushed up over my breasts. I just lay there in the sun with a hand on my belly and forget to care about everything else. That's my problem, I think. Ty makes my head fuzzy and unclear, like I'm stumbling through a dream when I'm with him. It's hard to focus on things like bills and jobs when he's walking around with his stupid nose ring and his butterfly tattoos. I sigh and reach up to steal Ty's unfinished cig, lighting it up and exhaling as I wait for him to come back. Because he always does. I don't ever mention this, and Ty doesn't either, but I know he still loves me more than anything in the world, and he always will. "I heart the fuck out of you," he tells our infant, and my smile turns into a grin. Our baby's first word is going to be fuck. I just know it is.

"When he wakes up, you want to go to the store?" Ty asks when he comes back outside, and I nod, watching as his shadow falls over me and makes me shiver. *God, Never, haven't you had enough?* I exhale and hold my hand up, so Ty can take his cigarette back.

"Sounds good," I say, wanting to move onto more serious matters, but having lost all of my earlier willpower. See, this is why I tried to get up early. Once Ty comes around, everything else just falls away. "I want a smoothie or something," I tell him as he sits down on the chair and pulls my feet into his lap. "Anything with strawberries in it, really." He passes the cig back and watches as I inhale.

"We should quit smoking," he tells me with serious eyes. I focus on the piercing in his left brow. It's silver today and matches the bangles on his arm and the rings on his fingers; it matches the one on my hand, the one with the blue stone. My wedding ring. I smile. Frown.

"We really should." Neither of us moves to stub out the crackling cherry.

"I talked to Beth this morning," he says nonchalantly. Ty talks to my sister more than I do. I don't know why; he just likes her I guess. "She was thinking the whole clan could come up here for Christmas."

I snort and Ty raises his eyebrow, his unpierced one.

"You don't want to see them?" he asks, but I'm already shaking my head, waving my cigarette around as I exhale.

"I do," I tell him, and I try not to sound upset that it's been so long. They've had shit going on; we've had shit going on. Things have been complicated. I don't tell Ty that I'm sad Beth wasn't here when I had my baby, and I don't tell him that I'm sad that I wasn't there when she had hers. We meant to be, but life just fucked everything all up. I wonder briefly what Noah thinks about our naming our kid after him. I talked to him just before Mini McCabe was born, but not after. I don't say anything to Ty, but I do miss him a little. As a friend, of course. Zella's still had no luck with him, but I don't think she's given up either. "But they won't make it. They'll try, but getting everybody out here would be next to impossible. We should probably just go down there. We're long overdue for another visit anyway." Ty watches me and smiles but doesn't say anything else about it.

"Are you happy, Never?" he asks me instead, and the question surprises me because it comes from seemingly out of nowhere. As if the weather can sense the shift in the mood, the clouds roll over the sun and tiny droplets of water begin to fall from the sky. The dog lifts her head up and barks once before retreating up the stairs and into the back door. The cat, on the other hand, comes darting out. Ty looks at me with those eyes and pierces me with that gaze, and I want to just blurt out that I am, but I don't know if that's entirely true. Some days it is, and others it's not. I'm always happy with Ty, and we don't often fight, but …

"I'm scared," I tell him, and he reaches out right away, taking my hand in his ringed one, curling his fingers tight around me.

"Why?" Neither of us gets up to go inside. The rain starts to pour. I watch as Ty's ebony hair falls into his eyes and sheds droplets down his cheeks, along the tip of his nose. "You know I'd never let anything or anyone come between us."

"I know," I whisper, and my voice is hard to hear over the sound of wetness cascading around us. My cigarette goes out and I toss it into the grass.

"Then what's wrong? I know this place isn't a palace, but it's … I'm trying to make it a home for you, for Noah." Tears fall from my wide eyes, but I don't let Ty know they're there. I pretend it's just rain, just cold droplets of fallen sky. I don't know how to explain how I feel to Ty. I've been trying, but it's not easy. I open my mouth to speak when my eye catches on the laptop.

"Shit!" I grab the computer with one hand and pull my shirt down with the other. Ty picks up the baby monitor and follows me inside, letting the screen door fall closed behind us. I swipe droplets off the smooth top with one hand and head into the kitchen to grab a dish towel. Noah begins to cry.

Ty watches me for a moment and then sets the monitor down on the table, moving up the stairs without another word. I want to follow after him and be a good mom and a good wife, but I'm not sure if I can. I've been feeling less and less adequate lately, like I'm not good enough to be the woman they both need. My back hits the cabinet, and I slide to the floor, setting the laptop down next to me and wrapping my arms around my knees. My boobs hurt like hell and I'm nauseous as fuck. Plus, my emotions have just fallen over the edge of the cliff and hit a horrible low. I'm supposed to be happy now. I have Ty and Noah; I've made up with most of my family, confronted Luis. But something is still missing and I'm not quite sure what it is.

I want to blame it on the house or the New York weather or the shitty buzzing noise that our fridge makes, but if I'm honest, I know that it's all coming from within: I don't feel like I deserve this perfect, fairytale ending. I want it, but I still don't believe that it's something Never Ross should be blessed with.

When I hear Ty coming down the stairs, I dash at my eyes with the back of my hand to make sure they're clear and stand up, taking the computer with me. I toss it onto the counter and start to prepare a bottle. When he steps into the kitchen, I'm smiling and pretending nothing wrong.

Neither of us acknowledges that he can see right through me.

4

Ty puts the baby carrier on this time and doesn't care that people give us looks over the bullet drawings. They don't get it, but we do. I hold back a secret smile.

We have to walk to the store because we don't have a car. The rental we had when we first arrived has long since been returned, but it hasn't mattered. We're not too far from the historic downtown area and haven't wanted for anything since we arrived. Except maybe my family. I've missed them like crazy, maybe even more so than the last time I left home. If money wasn't so tight, I'd have flown down there a dozen times already. More than once, I thought about asking Noah again, but I just couldn't do it. Pride wouldn't let me.

My eyes shift up and watch the gentle roil of autumn sky. The rain has stopped for now and doesn't seem like it'll be back for awhile. Just in case, we brought an umbrella anyway. It has an anarchy symbol on the top of it, courtesy of Ty's storage unit back in Cali. Lacey shipped all of that over to us, too – and paid for it. It surprises me sometimes that I ended up with good people around me. I spent so long feeling alone and lost that I'm having a hard time dealing with being found.

"Okay, so," Ty begins as I reach over and take his hand, squeezing it tighter than an afternoon walk would normally warrant. I just need him to feel me here with him, to know that even though I didn't quite answer his question, that I fucking love him so much it hurts. He returns the squeeze and gives me a dimpled smile. I know the subject isn't over yet, but I'm glad he isn't making a big deal out of it either. "We need toilet paper, formula, diapers … " I watch him cradling our kid's head with one hand, holding mine with the other. He's dressed in a yellow Sexual Obsession Group T-shirt, the one that says *Get SOGgy. Sexual obsession is a disease. Find your cure today.* I think that it's fitting considering that we're each other's cure. "Shampoo, milk, cereal," Ty continues, looking like a walking razor blade, sharp and deadly, sexy but dangerous. Even in this domestic setting, he looks wild. I pretend I don't notice when other women check him out, but I do, and I get a perverse pleasure out of it. "And condoms." Ty gives me a look and I bite my lip.

"Yeah, that would probably be good," I say, thinking about how bad we've been about using them. This sort of attitude is going to get us in trouble again. I don't count the number of unprotected sex sessions we've had in the past few weeks.

"Want to get a goodie?" Ty asks randomly, running his tongue across his lips and casting a glance my way that makes my body hot and soaks my shirt with sweat. He may as well be focusing a fucking laser my way. I try to return his look with one of my own, and feel satisfied when he smirks and swipes his left hand through his hair.

"What kind of goodie?"

"Like a toy or some shit," he tells me, taking his hand from mine and pretending to cover Noah's ears. "Something to make up for having to use a rubber. A vibrator or anal beads or a swing." I laugh, and it feels good, too good. I should've known that this little up was going to brief, that by the time evening rolled around, I'd be sitting in the bathroom sobbing. I'm just marked by the universe to be shit on.

"A swing?" I ask, trailing the end of the umbrella against the sidewalk. We've just hit the first of the shops and are starting towards the grocery store at the end of the block. Oddly enough, in this mix of taffy shops and clothing boutiques, there's a sex shop called *Fluttering Lashes* with lingerie in the front and naughty stuff in the back. We've only been in there once, and we took Noah with us. People stared and whispered, but neither of us gave a shit. We still don't. If we're going to buy a sex toy, we're going to walk in there with our baby and buy one. "How about a cock ring?"

"How about whatever you want?"

"I want you," I say and he grins.

"I fucking love you," he replies, and we continue on in silence, wrapped in naughty thoughts. I've never used a sex toy of any kind with a partner before. One night stands don't usually yield the opportunity to whip out a strap on and ask your partner if he's into anal. I glance over at Ty from under a wave of my hair. I bet he's used just about everything in the book, but I'm not going to ask. I don't want to know.

When we hit the store, we divide and conquer. Ty goes for food and I hit the personal aisles, grabbing our baby supplies, the shampoo, the toilet paper. I decide that I'll probably need some tampons soon and pick those up on my way to the condoms. On the top shelf, pregnancy tests stare down at me with nasty, little smirks. I don't think I need any, but I grab a box to use just in case. It's always nice to be sure and it doesn't hurt to check every once in awhile.

When Ty and I meet back up and he sees this on the belt, he gives me a look.

"No," I say before he can even ask. "It's just another level of precaution."

And that, of course, is just more ignorant, wishful thinking.

5

When we get back to the house, I end up with horrible cramps and decide to curl up on our bed with Noah tucked in next to me. Ty leaves us there and continues his work on the room across from ours. It's the most densely packed with items, many of them in pretty good condition. This is also the room where Ty's mother stored most of their family photos. Every once in awhile, McCabe comes in and flashes me a photo of him as a child. Sometimes, when I peek in on him, I see him sitting there and staring at something with a blank stare. I don't ever ask about those pictures.

I turn the pages of my novel with one hand and use the other to hold my strawberry smoothie, the one Ty got for me when even I had forgotten my craving. Ever since I got pregnant with Noah, I've been obsessed with strawberries. I keep wondering when it'll pass.

"Hey Nev," Ty says a while later, when I've finally turned the last page of my novel and been hit with the biggest book hangover *ever.* Sometimes I think it's possible for a book to be too good. If it's bad, who cares if it's over? "Is Noah asleep?" I look down and examine my son's face. It's round and pudgy, too cute to be a product of Ty and me. We're both so ... fucked up, and Noah is just ... just Noah. I touch his cheek with the back of my hand.

"Yeah, I think so," I say as Ty tiptoes in and slides his inked hands under the baby's body, picking him up so softly, so gently that he doesn't wake. Ty's bracelets jingle merrily, but they don't bother Noah. I think he associates that sound with his father already. I imagine that it's more comforting than anything else. "Be right back," he whispers. "I got a present for you."

I raise my eyebrows and watch him go, sitting up and stretching, wondering what he could possibly have gotten in our brief time apart. Ty and I rarely spend any time apart, not even when we're here at home. Always, always we're together, pulled close by a magnetic force that pushes and pulls that makes us feel safe and dangerous at the same time, ignites the soul and cools the heart. *I love that fucking man.*

I brush my fingers over the corner of my book as I wait, my mind drifting from one subject to another. *I need to go back to school. Ty needs to go to school. Noah needs us to go to school. But how do we make this work? How do we get through this?* Sometimes I think that I'm too young to have a kid and then I get paralyzed by fear. This is almost one of those moments, but as usual, Ty steps in to save me.

A purple, plastic bag hits the end of the bed near my feet. I glance at it and realize where it's from. The sex shop downtown.

"You fucking bastard," I whisper, but I'm smiling already. "You said you had trouble finding the Cheerios. I knew that was a load of bullshit."

"Nah, I was just having trouble finding the cock rings. They were hidden on a display between the glass dildos and the rabbit vibes." I laugh as I pull my gift up with my toe, grabbing it in greedy hands and dumping the contents out on the bed next to me. It's like a naughty bag of party favors for that birthday party where only you're invited. "Did you get the condoms?" he asks me, and I nod.

"They're in the bathroom."

Ty disappears for a moment to retrieve the box while I dig through the items he purchased. He did, indeed, grab a cock ring along with a pair of lacy, crotchless panties, and some flavored lube. It's not a lot, but it's enough. It's always enough with Tyson Monroe McCabe. Just the gesture is fucking cute.

When Ty returns, he's already naked and has a condom between his teeth. I watch as he adjusts the volume on the baby monitor and switches off the overhead light, leaving us with the dim lighting from the lamp on the nightstand. When he grabs it in two fingers and winks at me, I know I'm in trouble.

"We can't just fuck all the time," I tell him, not because I want to start a fight or anything but because I have to distract myself from his hard body. I swear, the man never works out, but he manages to keep a fucking six pack and pecs like rocks. His arms are colorful swarms of brightness, fluttering over the rounded curves of his bicep and blending into the winged flock across his upper back. When he comes to me, I run my fingers over the back of his neck and the tattoo that's there, branding him as mine. *Never say Never.* I smile. "We do have to think about practical things once in a while."

"Really?" he asks, brushing a kiss along my jaw and rolling over me, landing on the bed next to me, erection pointing up at the ceiling, begging me to grab on and take control of it. But tonight, Ty doesn't want me to take control. Just by looking in his eyes, I can tell. "Says who?" I watch as he rips open the package and pulls out the condom, giving it a distasteful glare before he slips it into his cock. I watch, mesmerized, and he knows it. My eyes narrow, but they don't stray.

"You know," I say, ignoring his question. He knows what has to be done. I can't doubt that. Ty won't let anything happen to our new family. I'm not a sniveling, little bitch who's incapable of taking care of herself, but at the same time, I know Ty has that old school responsibility thing going on. He's a real man and he'll take care of us like a real man should. I just hope I can match up to him and be a real woman for our family. As of now, I think I'm falling short. "If you hadn't been so opposed to these things," I flick my fingers in the direction of his dick, but I don't touch it, not yet. I'm already soaked down there and my thighs are rubbing against one another in anticipation. "We wouldn't have had a baby ten months after meeting each other in a seedy bar." Ty laughs at me and strokes his hand down his shaft, using the lube from the condom to keep it nice and slick. My tongue runs across my lower lip.

"Then I guess we made a good decision, huh?" Ty slides

his hand over my belly and grabs the underwear, picking them up with a single finger. "Now be a good girl and put your panties on."

"Go to hell," I tell him, but I stand up, enjoying this feeling of being sexy for Ty, of being free. I strip my shirt and bra off, drop my jeans to the floor. While Ty pleasures himself, I change out my boyshorts for the crotchless panties. "These are fucking ridiculous, you know?" I tell him. He darts forward suddenly and grabs me by the wrist, pulling me onto the bed and rolling on top of me in a single motion. His bracelets jingle as he reaches out and switches off the lamp.

"Oh come on, Never," he whispers in the sudden darkness, leaning down, breathing against my forehead. "You know you like them. Easy access, right?"

"Easy access would mean going commando, Ty."

"Oh, I see, that's how it is," he growls at me as he reaches his hands up and caresses my swollen breasts. It's an almost painful pleasure – they're so sore and full and tender. I groan and grab onto Ty's hair, tugging it hard and drawing a moan from his throat. "You're going to school me on this shit."

"Doubtful," I tell him as he kisses one nipple and then the other. I have to swallow three times before I can speak again. "I've never used a cock ring before."

"Good," he says, and he rises up on his elbows and looks down at me. I can't see much of his face in this light, but I can feel him. He's a part of me now, a missing piece I never knew I was looking for until I found it. "I was about to get jealous and you don't want to see me jealous." I kiss his lips, taste his hot heat, pierce myself on the thorns of his heart and hope his poison kills me. "You're mine and there's nobody on this fucking earth that can change that," he tells me, moving down, pressing his lips against my stomach, biting my belly button ring and tugging on it gently with his teeth. Then he pauses and sits up, grabbing the cock ring and ripping open the package.

I watch as he stretches it wide with his fingers, the thinning, gray light from outside highlighting his hand for a brief moment before it disappears into the shadows as he slips it onto his cock.

"You might like this at first," he says, and I don't need to see the smirk on his face to know it's there. "But you might regret suggesting it to me later."

"And why's that?" I ask as Ty grabs me by the hips and turns me over, pressing his hardness against me, teasing that tender spot that's highlighted by the black lace that's cupping my ass cheeks on either side. It's hard to sound ornery when your butt is up in the air and your hands are clenched tight around the sheets, but I try.

"This, my sweet, baby mama, is a magical device. With this motherfucker wrapped around my cock, I can keep it up all night." And then he thrusts forward, not being so gentle this time. I cry out, but I don't tell him to stop; I can't. I want this; I want it so bad it hurts. I'm not going to admit it to anyone but myself, but all these weeks of McCabe being gentle with me have left me ... wanting. I'm glad that he's sweet, but I also like his sour. I want to lick it off like a fucking Sour Patch Kid.

When I try to move my right hand to my clit, he reaches down and grabs my wrist, traps it in his ringed fingers and slams it into my lower back.

"Oh no," he says, voice harsh and guttural, laced with pain. *What the fuck?* "You're not touching that, not yet. You don't want to finish too fast." And then he proceeds to fuck me so hard that it hurts, that I almost ask him to slow down, almost. Until I realize why he's doing this and what's wrong. I scared him today, when he asked me if I was happy. Before, I asked

Ty McCabe if he would run, if he would go off and fuck somebody behind my back, leave me. I never thought to wonder if he had the same fears about me. He may not even know why he's doing this, but I do. Ty is afraid, and I don't blame him.

"I love you," I tell him instead, and he pauses, freezes there with his body buried inside of mine, his hand pinning my wrist to my back.

"Still?" he asks. He doesn't let his voice change with the question, but I can feel the slight clench of his body, the contraction of his muscles.

"Always." Ty slides out of me and releases my arm, sitting back on his ankles. I turn over and look up at him, reaching for his neck, sighing when he presses his head into my throat.

"Fuck," he says, and he sounds hurt. Maybe a little uncomfortable, too. He does have a silicone ring wrapped around his erection after all, and I know it's not easy to stop. My body is screaming at me, begging me to ask Ty for another baby, for him to tear off his condom and spill himself in me. "Never, fuck," he says. And then he enters me, slides into the slickness and just holds there. "I didn't mean this for you. I didn't want you to have a hard life. I thought I was making up a good one for you."

"Ty," I begin, but he isn't ready to listen to me talk yet, doesn't know that my problems are all bone deep, started a long, long time ago when my father was taken away and my family chose not to believe me. It's not easy to have self-worth when you're not valued. Things are better now, yes, but the scars remain. I've come a long way, but I still have roads to travel, mountains to climb.

"Never," he says as I tangle my hands in his hair, squeeze him so tight that he grunts, body clenching as mine pulses around him, draws him in deep. "Whatever you need, you let me know, and I'll get it for you. I'll do fucking anything for you. I'll wade through knee-deep shit to make you happy. You know that, right?" Tears sting my eyes, but I don't respond. The only person that can get me through my newest set of bullshit is me. But if I tell Ty this, it'll freak him out. I keep it to myself, and use my grip on his hair to pull his lips to mine. When we kiss, I make him a promise with my mouth that this has nothing to do with him, that I love him more than breath, more than life, more than existence. I tell him without words that I'd rather blink out and become nothing than lose him.

But things will still be hard, and they'll still suck, and we'll still fight. We just have to get through the downs and live for the ups. I'm ready for the run; it'll be the little details that fuck me.

6

After Ty and I are finished, we lay in silence and smoke, watching curls of gray tease the tin ceiling and creep along the edges where the walls meet up with it. This time, I'm the one that gets out of bed and checks on Noah. I do it because I think Ty's starting to worry that I don't like our son, and that's not it at all. It's just ... weird. I don't think I was ready to be a mother, but I am one, and I have to get used to it.

I stand there with one hand on the edge of the crib, the other holding an unlit cigarette and feeling guilty for it. I've never felt guilty about smoking before, not really. But Noah makes me feel bad about it. It's not like I ever actually smoke around him, but I can't help but wonder if each cig I smoke is a day I lose with my son.

I touch my fingers to his cheeks and watch his chest rise and fall, dressed up in a fuzzy blue jumper. Tears bite at my eyes again, and I feel sick with myself.

"Never," Ty says, gliding into the room on silent feet. He wraps his arms around my waist, teasing my nostrils with the smell of tobacco. "Please don't be sad."

"I'm not," I tell him. "Well, not all the time. I'm just … I feel really emotional right now. It's probably just hormones. I'm about to start my period." I pull my hand away from Noah and turn to see the skeptical look on Ty's face. I'm failing again, and it sucks. I don't want him to feel the way he's feeling. I'm such a fucking cunt, stealing away the joy in Ty's eyes when he's with his kid. Any displeasure I show around Noah will make Ty resent him, and I could never, ever do that. But I know I'm first in his eyes, always. And it isn't cruel; it's just right. Parents should love each other more than they love their kids, should be there to create a solid foundation for them to stand out, so that when they go out in the world they know there are two people who will do anything for them. I want Noah to know what a good relationship is like, and I want him to find one. Ty is my prize. He is my win. He's the one thing I wanted to get out of this life.

"I'm going to take a piss," I tell him and he laughs, voice echoing around the quiet house. Outside, the rain's started up again. We waves his hand at me, jingling his bangles around in a mimicry of the wind chimes that are screaming in the wind in our backyard.

"That's hot, Nev, thanks for sharing that with me." I don't mention that he already has another erection.

In the bathroom, I sit down on the toilet and notice absently that the bag of items from the store is sitting on the counter. The pregnancy tests and the tampons are sticking out of the plastic, teasing me like a cruel joke. I don't know that quite yet. All I fucking know is that I'm going to try to be more responsible, be a fucking adult. So I grab the flowery box and pull out a test, sticking it underneath me for the hell of it. Just to see it turn negative, to know that we're okay.

I set the plastic stick on the counter and grab my toothbrush, spreading a line of minty gel on the top and thanking the universe that I don't have to use a miswak anymore. *Fuck you, Angelica,* I think as I brush my teeth and stand up, flushing the toilet and spitting into the sink. I pick up the pregnancy test and glance absently at it.

My eyes go wide; my heart stops.

Right. Fuck. I don't really know why I'm surprised. I guess I sort of assumed that getting pregnant a few weeks after you gave birth was not a possibility. What a sick, sick joke for the universe to play. It's perverse. Mental. Fucked.

My pulse races so hard that I get dizzy and end up sitting on the floor.

You think you'd have learned by now, Never. You don't use a condom, you have a baby. God, you're awfully ignorant for someone who's fucked like, a hundred people. Get it together, woman.

I lean over the toilet and throw up. The stick hits the floor and bounces a few times before coming to rest in the shadows.

"This is not happening," I whisper to myself, voice echoing around the porcelain bowl. A second later, Ty bursts in looking worried. When he sees me bent over, he kneels down and touches his hand to my forehead. I'm soaked in sweat, just dripping.

"Jesus fucking Christ," he says in his stupid freaking stud way. I knew it. I knew a *look* from that man could get me pregnant. Screwing him without a condom is just asking trouble. I'm surprised Noah was part of a sextuplet or something. I grip the seat hard and do my best not to think about the way it looked when we first cleaned it out – covered in fucking feces, filled to the brim with *cat litter.* My stomach roils again. "Are you alright? Should I call an ambulance? I'm calling an ambulance." Ty stands up and tries to move away, but I grab him around the ankle, my hand pale and slick.

"No," I say, and my voice is firm, unwavering. Wouldn't that just be a peach? He calls 911 and asks them to come out because I'm having a panic attack about being *pregnant.* Ty pauses and squats back down behind me, sticking a cigarette in his mouth. Sometimes, I think he's even worse than me when it comes to smoking.

"You sure?" he mumbles, his cig dancing around and teases the flame of the lighter he produces in his hands. I'm not, but I don't tell him that. Yet. My hand drops to the tiled floor and fumbles around, searching for the test. Ty watches me, but he doesn't move.

"Ross," he warns, but I ignore him, belly muscles clenching tight as I dry heave again. *How attractive is this? Like it wasn't bad enough having him see me spread-eagled in stirrups at the hospital. One day, I'm going to run out of sexy tokens, and he's going to look at me and think,* What the fuck? Tears start again which kind of just pisses me off. Which makes me cry more. I angry cry the shit out of that toilet and do my best not to scream. Well. Guess that means I'm not crazy. My mood swings are all thanks to Ty's seed. His fertile, fucking seed.

"I hate you," I tell to him to which he responds by

shrugging and falling back onto his ass. The smell of tobacco mixes with the scent of puke. I slam my hand down and flush the toilet.

"Let me guess," he begins, and he's smiling even though it's not funny. Even though the last thing we need is another baby. I can barely handle the one. I start to panic. "Bad smoothie?"

"This isn't funny, Ty!" I scream as my fingers finally close around the test. I throw it at his face and don't even care that there's pee on it. Serves him right. I slump back against the cabinet and wrap my hands around my head. I don't want to be pregnant again. Being pregnant sucks unless you're Beth Regali. *Stupid bitch. Tramping around and 'glowing'. I hate her.*

Ty takes his cig out with his ringed fingers and picks up the test with his other hand. He looks at it for about five minutes before he speaks.

"Shit."

That's all he says.

"You think?" I whisper, soaking the front of my shirt with liquid. I'm glad it's dark in here, so Ty can't see. I don't want him to see. Above all things, I want him to be happy. *I* just want to make him happy.

"This is for sure?" My head snaps up, and I throw him my worst glare. Doesn't phase him a bit. "These things aren't always accurate, right?" I keep staring. He can't see my face, but he can feel me. Ty always knows what I'm thinking. Sometimes it bugs me, feels like he's so deep in my head that my thoughts aren't just my own. Usually, I like it. Right now, I want to stab him with a miswak. Sorry, toothbrush. A sharp one.

"You're kidding, right?" I ask him. He's asking, but he doesn't seem surprised, not really. "And how is it you're not upset about this?" Ty looks at the test and takes a drag on his cig. When I crawl across the bathroom floor and try to snatch it from him, he keeps his fingers tight.

"Never." I drop my hand with a groan and lean my head against his bare belly. I hear a fizzle and a plop as he tosses the cig into the toilet.

"We're so stupid," I moan as Ty's hand strokes my hair softly. His bracelets tinkle with each movement, lighting up the room with a metallic chorus. "Like, on the verge of being mentally handicapped."

"Nah, baby," he says, pulling me into him, squeezing me tight. I still think he smells like danger, pain, heartache, but it's intoxicating, so I don't mind. "When we're around each other, we just get lost in each other. That's not a crime, is it?"

"I don't want another baby."

Ty thinks about this for a moment.

"Okay," he tells me, but he doesn't sound sure. I snuggle into him hard, force him to hold me up, to take care of me. I feel bad, but it's been a long time since I had someone to do it, and he seems willing enough. I guess maybe I should be comforting him, too, but he doesn't seem upset. Oh yeah, and his tits don't hurt. I put two hands over my stomach and try to breathe. "Whatever you want, I'll be there for you." I hear a frown in his voice. "But I can tell you a secret?"

"If it isn't about condoms, I don't want to hear it."

Ty laughs at this.

"I like you being pregnant."

"Oh, for fuck's sake," I say. I try to sit up for maximum glaring capability, but he won't let me go. Ty will Never let me go. "You want me barefoot and pregnant, dropping babies across the floor as I clean?"

"Oh no, fuck that. All I'm saying is, I like knowing I've got all of you."

"You'll always have all of me," I tell him. The words sound lovey-dovey, but they're not. Right now, I'm just irritated. I do my best to keep the wetness of my tears off Ty's stomach, but a few stray ones fall anyway.

"I know. I just like the proof, you know? Makes me feel all manly and shit."

"You're an asshole."

"But an asshole that loves the fuck out of you."

"I want an abortion." Ty pauses for a moment, and I can tell he doesn't. But if that's what I want, he'll help me through it. I know he will. "Maybe. Or not. I don't know. I don't want to make this decision."

"And for that, I really am sorry." His voice is grave when he says this. A few silent moments pass before either of us speaks again. "But you're just so damn cute." He's trying to make a joke. I appreciate that, but I don't laugh. I can't. Not when I'm this angry with myself. What's the saying? The definition of insanity is doing the same thing over and over again, and expecting different results.

Unprotected sex = babies. That's life. That's nature.

"If you do want to have the baby, know that I'll take the load off of you however I can."

"I want to go back to school," I whisper. Ty's lips come down and meet the edge of my forehead, brushing against my hair, bringing goose bumps to my skin.

"No more fucking around," he promises. "We'll come up with a game plan. Everything will be okay. There's no way it couldn't be. Long as I'm with you, the world can go fuck itself."

I want to believe him. I do. I do, but I can't. Not yet.

There are still a lot of things that could go wrong. So many, many things.

7

"Never, what were you fucking thinking?"

I hear a slap as Beth cups a hand over her mouth and drops her voice to a whisper.

"I'm sorry," she says quickly. "I have no room to talk, really. It's … I know it's harder than it sounds." I sneak a drag of my cigarette and look over my shoulder to make sure that Ty's not on his way down the stairs. I'm standing on the front porch in an oversized shirt with no panties, having what I keep promising myself is my last cigarette. It might not be good for the baby, but it also wouldn't be good for her or him if I were to die from a heart attack either.

"No, Beth," I say as I watch Chuck put a claw into the tip of Angelica's nose. The dog yelps and comes crawling over to me for protection. "It's pretty fucking easy. The rubber goes over that hard bit between their legs, and when they cum, it traps their baby sauce."

"Never, that's disgusting," she tells me, and I can just imagine her hiding outside on the porch the same way as me, glancing around to make sure none of the kids can hear our conversation. Especially the cursing bits.

"Or I could've just popped a pill. It really isn't that hard."

"It's … complicated. Boys like Ty … " I know her mind is drifting to Danny Delphino, but he is nowhere near Tyson Monroe McCabe. Not even freaking close. If Ty's a stallion, Mr. Delphino would rank right up around the status of donkey fucker.

"They burn like fire? Curl tendrils of smoke around your logical mind and choke it to death?" Beth laughs, but I don't think it's very funny. Not that I really blame Ty. I mean, come on. This was an inevitable conclusion with a predictable outcome. "So what do I do?"

"You know I can't answer that question for you," she tells me, and I know, somehow, that she's thinking of our mother, wondering where we'd be if Angelica had done a better job by us.

"Beth, I suck at being a mom."

"I don't believe that for an instant," she says as my hand drops and traces my dog's velvety ear. She seems to sense that something is wrong and sits right on my feet, looking up at me with her head tilted to one side, leaning into my stroking fingers. "It's all about love. You know that. Just be the opposite of mom, and you'll be alright." Beth chuckles, but I don't.

"How is everyone?" I ask, phone tucked between my ear and shoulder, so I can hold my cigarette. I stare at it for awhile and imagine what Beth would say if she knew. I'm pretty damn sure she'd crucify me. Suddenly, I hear footsteps on the stairs and end up chucking the burning cherry through the air. It spins end over end and comes to rest on the pathway leading up the house. "Shit, sorry, hold that thought. I gotta go." I hang up before she can answer and rush down the steps, bending down to grab the cig and snub it out in the gravel.

"Um, can I respectfully ask that you get your ass the fuck over here?" Ty asks, looking at me bent over with no panties on in the front yard. Oops. I stand up and throw him a glare, walking back to the porch nonchalantly.

"What's your problem?"

"My problem," he says, coming down to meet me, grabbing me around the waist with one arm and hiking my shirt up so the cool air kisses my naked cheeks. "Is that I don't want any motherfuckers driving down the block and scoping out my wife's tight, little ass."

"Say it again," I warn him as he drags me close, presses his mouth to my temple and exhales in a hiss. My body goes limp. See, this is what he does to me. I can't think. Okay, well I can think but only about him bending me over right here and now and fucking the shit out me. Condoms? What condoms?

"*Wife*," he growls and my heart thumps painfully against my chest, comes up against my ribs to meet his. I can hear it pounding from here. He breathes molten lava against my neck, teasing my jaw with his teeth, kissing my mouth so hard that it hurts. A car drives by, and I'm pretty damn sure it slows down. I would, too, I think if I saw too gnarly little demons making out in the front yard – one, shirtless, the other, pant-less.

I push away and close my eyes, trying to contain myself.

"The baby?" I ask him, keeping my gaze focused on the screen door.

"Awake and ready to see you," he says in his charcoal voice. We don't bring up the pregnancy yet. It's too early in the AM for that. I smile sadly and pull away reluctantly. I feel like I'm letting Noah down by being pregnant again, like somehow I'm taking something away from him. I think of my sisters and how close together we are in age. *Like mother like daughter.* My sad smile becomes a scowl, and I'm glad Ty's behind me and can't see it. My sisters are blessings and curses both. I can't imagine not having them, yet I can also imagine that if I had gotten more attention, had loving parents, how easy my life could've been. Ugh. I just want to pull out my fucking hair.

"Hey there, Mr. Ross," I say, reaching into the crib and pulling out the little warm body, tucking him under my chin and breathing in deep.

"McCabe," says Ty from the doorway. He doesn't mention the cigarette I smoked, but I know he knows. I can't hide anything from the man.

"Ross-McCabe," I correct. I turn to look at him, and we both smile. Mine turns into a sigh which turns into a nagging worry and that horrible feeling of not being good enough. Not enough. I am *not* enough for these two wonderful boys, so how can I add someone else into this mix? How can I, in good conscious, bring someone else into this world when I'm not even sure how to navigate it anymore? I hold Noah close and rub his back in small circles.

"So, I was talking to Beth last night," Ty begins, and I have to raise my eyebrows and give him a *look*.

"You two best friends now or something?" I ask and he smiles.

"She's the mother-in-law I always wanted," he says, no hint of a joke in his voice. I step up to him and tug on his nose ring. "I refuse to acknowledge the bitch that gave birth to you."

"Good," I tell him, leaning in and letting him hold us both in his strong arms. "I have to agree with that. Maybe one day, if she comes to me and apologizes, I'll forgive her. For now, my best bet is to pretend she doesn't exist." Ty's fingers squeeze my arm gently and his breath exhales in a rush. I know that he's thinking about his mom now, that he thinks about her almost everyday that we're here. I believe that living in this house is helping to come with things, like he's communicating with her by just being here. The house was a wreck, but I know there are little things, picture albums and dress shirts and crocheted pillows, that speak to him in a soft voice, tell him she wasn't all bad. I think he likes that. And I know there are horrible memories here, despicable ones, but he's dealing with that, too, paving over them with new ones – me, Noah, the farmer's market, the stupid tabby cat. "So what did you talk with Beth about?"

"Going down there," he says, and before I can protest that he doesn't have the money, that *we* don't have the money, he adds, "Permanently. Or at least for a little while, until we figure out what we want to do next."

"What?" I ask, stepping back, looking up into his face. "I thought you wanted to stay here? Keep this house? Make a life?"

"I have a life wherever I am, as long as I'm with you Never Fontaine Regali-Ross-McCabe. We'll sell the house, if we can. It's free and clear, so whatever we get would help. And I know you've been missing your sisters like crazy. I'm such a fuckwad for making you stay here. I wanted to be in the house out of some screwed up quest for redemption or some shit. Like, if I could make it work here, I could make it work anywhere, and I'd be free of all the guilt for … everything. I kinda made this house an analogy for my soul, you know? Fix it up on the outside and on the inside, everything will fall into place." Ty touches the side of my face with his knuckles, flutters the orange and black butterfly on the back of his hand against my skin. He smiles and his brown eyes twinkle, making me feel weak in the fucking knees. He might be a dad now, and a married man, but he still has that power to drop women to their knees with a single glance. I do my best not to sigh contentedly. That wouldn't exactly be in my character, now would it? "It took me awhile, but even a dense shithead such as myself gets it after awhile. If I'm with you, and Noah, and whoever it is that this may or may not be." Ty puts his hand on my belly and gives me a smoldering look. "I am fucking whole and everything else doesn't mean shit."

"Eloquently put," I tell him, but despite all the cursing and the sexual ardor infused into his words, Ty always makes sense. He's profane but wise. I love that about him. I think that's one of the things that set him apart from the other boys I was with, the ones who had pasts just as hot, just as vulnerable and unstable, crackling like a soon-to-be explosion. They still didn't get it, not even after all they'd been through. They cussed, too, (in the few, small brief conversations I ever had with any of them) though probably not as much, but all they talked about where parties and drinking and drugs and girls and fucking and sports. They didn't have bracelets and they didn't wear rings and they sure as shit didn't speak in quotable quotes worthy of slapping onto the side of a mug or the front of a T-shirt.

Ty watches me, watches these thoughts move across my eyes and then kisses me gently on the lips before I can protest.

"I know what you're going to say, but don't. This isn't my dream; you are. I don't care about this house; I care about you. Let's sell it and start over, wherever you want. In the South, the West, the North fucking Pole. Despite my previous, precarious position, I have sick ass fucking credit. I can buy you another house. You can go back to school."

"Promise me you'll never do a job that kills your soul, one that breaks you, promise me you'll never … " I don't need to finish that sentence. *Promise me you'll never use your body to get by in this world. It isn't worth it. It never was.* I know Ty said he was done with that, and I believe him, but I know his love delves deep and if it came down to feeding his family, he'd do whatever it took. He looks at me for a long, long while.

"I promise," he says, easy, just like that. I smile. Noah starts to cry. Ty grins and kisses his head, grabbing me by the hand and pulling us down the stairs. Neither of us speaks while he prepares a bottle and hands it to me. "I had fun here, though," he tells me, and I know that's true. He points down at Chuck Norris. "And I'm taking the cat."

I smile back at him.

"And the dog." We both glance over at Angelica. My mother must know by now that we named a bitch after her. Fitting, I think, she is one. I'm sure my little sisters delighted in telling her, unaware that they were probably pushing her to the edge of a tantrum.

"So you're in?" he asks. I think for a minute, gazing at my son, his cheeks, his pretty hazel eyes. I was almost positive he was going to end up with copper hair, but I guess Ty's genes felt the need to bully in there, mark him with a bit of that beautiful blackness that's in both of our souls. I wonder if this move would help me feel better, if I could get over this stupid fuck ass slump and figure out why I'm not as happy as I should be. If it will help me decide whether or not to keep my second baby. I don't have to think very long.

"I'm in."

8

We pack up all the stupid shit we had shipped out here in the first place, get ready send it back home with Beth's blessing. I can't help but wonder how my mother feels about all of this, if she even cares. She hasn't asked once about her grandkid.

Ty's already spoken with a realtor, and they have somebody that wants to see the house. One week on the market and the old rambler is drawing attention. Not too fucking shabby. This house does have character, I think, as I glance up at the tin ceiling, the crown molding, the fading wallpaper. If someone with money were to come in here and flip it, it would probably be pretty fabulous. As of right now, it's kind of a shack. But it's our shack. I put a hand on my lip and try not to get nostalgic. We're only been here, what, ten months? Eleven? I shake my head and go back to my task.

I'm cleaning out our closet, pulling my boxes of belly dancing costumes out and pausing to wipe a hand across my face. I still haven't danced for Ty yet. I've meant to, but I just haven't had the opportunity. Now that I'm pregnant again, I don't know if I'm going to be able to for awhile. Scratch that, going to want to for awhile. It's not like I *couldn't*, but I doubt that I will.

I kick the box aside and it jingles. Noah coos happily, and I can't hold back a smile. I'm pretty sure his reaction as more to do with his father than anything else. The jingling of the belly dance costumes mimic the ring of Ty's bracelets, and I think the reason he falls asleep so fast when Ty rocks him to sleep is because of that jewelry. The soft clatter of metal is actually pretty fucking comforting. Hey, it works for me and my black soul just fine.

I push my way into the closet and reach behind the row of old coats that Ty's mom left, back to a plastic garment bag that's hanging behind them. I manage to wrangle it out and notice that it's not covered in dust like the rest of the crap. It's as clear and clean as the belly dance boxes I put in there a few months ago.

"What the fuck is this, Mini McCabe?" I ask as I unzip it and reveal a dress. A white dress. A *wedding* dress. Holy shit. Holy shitting shitting shit. I fling the bag on the bed and scoot past the baby who's sitting on the floor in a car seat. The plastic spreads open and the dress comes out, draping over my hands like water, fluid and liquid, pure as freshly fallen snow. Angelic. Virginal. Until I turn it over and see that the lacing on the back is red, blood red. It's the most beautiful fucking thing I have ever seen (as far as inanimate objects go).

More tears come, and I have no choice but to blame them on the pregnancy, so I can keep my dignity and my tough as nails badass bitch persona.

When I hear Ty coming up the stairs, I stash the dress under the bed turn Noah so that he can watch me as I run into the bathroom and throw up. Apparently, I'm going to get blessed with morning sickness again. Nice. Anything that stirs up my nerves for any reason gets me to upchuck in the damn toilet. Jesus.

"You okay, baby?" he asks me, coming in and sweeping my hair back, smelling like the cigarettes we're *both* supposed to be giving up now. I nod, but say nothing. I'm afraid I speak, I'll blurt some Hallmark card bullshit, something that belongs in cursive pink text. "I was thinking, if you wanted, we could probably leave as soon as Friday." Again, I nod. "We'll get some kennels for the animals and maybe toss your son in there to save on airfare. I don't think he'd mind riding down with the cargo, do you?" I nod. I'm not really listening, and Ty knows it. He flushes the toilet for me and helps me to my feet. When I make eye contact with him, he raises his brows.

"What?"

"You're not all there. What's wrong? You just told me it was chill to throw your son in a kennel with the dog." I roll my eyes and push away from Ty, stepping back into the bedroom, watching the sunshine stream through the window and across our bed. Ty grabs me around the waist and leans down to whisper in my ear. "You're hiding something from me. What is it?" I shake my head. Whatever it is that Ty was going to do with that dress is important to me. I don't want to spoil the surprise.

"I'm just … curious. To see where we're going, where we'll end up."

I move towards the window and look down, into the yard and across the street, at the copse of trees that block our view of the neighbor's house and yard. Ty follows me over and trails his fingers across the skin on my upper back, my neck.

"As soon as you have this baby, we've got to get you a tattoo, one that says *Property of Ty McCabe.*"

"Go to hell," I tell him as he steps back and pauses. The way he freezes tells me right away that something's wrong. For a second, I think something's wrong with Noah, that he's just suffered from SIDS and is gone forever. Pain crashes over me, but when I spin around, I see that he's okay, that Ty isn't even looking at him. Nausea sweeps over me.

Ty bends down and grabs the bit of fabric that's poking out from under the bed. Shit. The white dress follows and then he's smiling, looking up at me, eyes half-lidded.

"Never."

"I found it when I was cleaning," I say.

"Never."

I cross my arms over my chest, prepared to argue. I don't know why. Maybe it's just conditioned in me, put there by having too many sisters. Argument is a fact of life, a daily occurrence when you've got that many girls in one house.

"What is this, Ty?"

"What do you think it is?" he asks me, setting the dress down, glancing at Noah. The baby is now fast asleep. He moves forward and grabs the hem of my shirt. I clamp my hands down on his wrists, right over his bracelets and glare.

"But why do you have this?" I ask. Ty's smile becomes a grin and then the shirt is just coming up and over my head. Before I can protest, he's got the dress back in his hands, lifting it up, looking coy as hell.

"Try it on?" he asks. "For me."

"That's cheap."

"Talk's cheap. I thought you loved me?"

"Haha," I say, shaking my hand, raising my hands up with a sigh. The dress comes down and kisses my skin, fucks me softly, teases my flesh. "Happy? Now explain." Ty takes my face in his hands and kisses me.

"I was going to build an archway, cover it in black roses, and marry the shit out of your ass in the yard. But since we're moving, I guess I'm going to have to settle for fucking the shit out of you in it instead."

"You owe me a suit." Ty snaps his fingers and starts to undress. I watch him and follow suit, dropping my jeans to the floor beneath the dress. When he goes to the dresser buck naked, and throws a tie around his neck, I almost swoon. Almost. But Never Ross doesn't swoon. She has a mean glare though. "This is not a suit."

"It's better than a suit," he says, coming to me, kissing me, caressing. It's a suit that gives you easy access to my dick."

"Romantic."

"Always."

"So now what?"

"Now," he asks, crooking an eyebrow, glancing down at his son to make sure he's sleeping soundly enough to get through Mommy and Daddy's debauchery. "Now we play a little game called *Here Cums the Bride.*"

9

The next morning, Ty and I get dressed and put Noah in his baby carrier, getting ready to leave, so the realtor can show the house. He's promised me a strawberry smoothie if I cooperate, so I go along willingly, trying not to smile when I think of the crumpled white dress I've hung back up in the closet. Might have some stains on it now, too. I guess it isn't so virginal and perfect anymore. I grin.

We're running late and only make it about halfway down the block when we see her car. Ty waves; I don't. A minute later, a second car comes by. My eyes catch on the face of the woman inside and something about her seems familiar. I can't place her though and figure we've probably brushed elbows in the grocery store or something. I think this until I turn and see the expression on my young husband's face. He's white as a fucking ghost, and he's not walking anymore. He's standing there clutching his son with one hand, turning in a slow half circle and following the back of the car with wide eyes.

"The fuck?" he asks. I watch Ty bite his lip hard. The name that escapes his lips next sends chills down my spine. "Hannah."

"Hannah?" my voice comes out in a squeak, and I'm so fucking glad that Ty's the one holding our baby. "Hannah, the pedophile?" I ask, referring to the woman that took Ty's virginity, who paid him for sex when he was a thirteen year old runaway. I see red. "What in the goddamn fucking shit is that *whore* doing driving to my house?" My voice rises an octave with each word, and my heart pounds out a sharp, slicing bolero to the gods of war. Noah senses something is wrong and starts to cry.

"I don't … I have no fucking clue," Ty says. He sounds baffled, but not angry. Not yet. Or maybe that's because this time, it's my job. I start to run. "Never!" Ty shouts, but he's helpless to come after. Can't exactly take off at a pounding job with a newborn strapped to your chest. I pummel back down the sidewalk and into the yard just in time see Hannah climbing out of her car. It's a nice car, admittedly, far too nice for someone like her.

I come up and hit her hard, just after the realtor calls out a cheerful hello to me. Hannah falls back and slams into the shiny red paint of her sedan.

"Who the fuck do you think you are?" I growl, squeezing her biceps with my nails, digging them into her pale flesh.

Her pale lips are parted and her blue eyes are wide. "What is your fucking deal?"

"My deal?" she asks as the realtor stumbles over and looks between us, trying to decide if she should get involved or not. I slash a glare her way and she steps back. "I'm just here to look at the house. Who are you?" So she's playing dumb. Fine. Maybe this will wake her up. My fist comes back, but strong fingers grasp me around the wrist and keep me from making a stupid mistake, one that could end up with me sitting pregnant in prison.

"Mrs. McCabe," Ty says, and I think he chooses his words purposely. "Don't do something you'll regret." I want to tell him that I could never regret decking this bitch, that she deserves a good beat down, that I could *kill* her and not feel bad about it. I try to think of Ty and my kid and my sisters instead, turning away and rubbing my hands down my face.

"Hello there," Hannah says and the sound of her voice almost takes me over the edge, sends me into a wild rage. I bite my lip so hard it bleeds, trying to contain myself. From the backyard, Angelica starts to bark. "This is quite a coincidence."

"Oh, I'm sure," Ty says and his voice holds venom, thick and pungent. I turn around and watch their interaction. Inside of me, our new baby stirs. Or at least I imagine it does. In all reality, it's probably the size of a pea. I put a hand over my stomach and hold my ground. "Hannah, I don't think I need to tell you how weird this is." Hannah brushes her honeyed curls back. She looks the picture of innocence standing there in a green and yellow sundress, hair fluttering softly in the wind. Perfect facade for a child fucker.

"I'm looking to buy a house, Tyson." She smiles; my red rage turns violet. "How was I supposed to know this one was yours?"

"Sorry, bitch, we don't sell to pedophiles. Take your freak show on the road."

"Excuse me," the realtor says, trying to interject herself between Hannah and me. When I flash my gaze over to her though, she shrinks back a bit. She's weak. I consider telling her to grow a backbone, but I know I'm just being mean. I focus my rage back on Hannah.

"I don't really appreciate you speaking to me like that," she says, voice so soft it's nearly ripped away by the wind. I see her eyes fall on Mini McCabe and I come *this* close to strangling her. I step forward, Ty steps to the side and puts his hand over my chest. When he tosses a glance back at me, he's smiling. No dimples and it doesn't reach his eyes, but it's there.

"Hey you."

I don't know how to respond to that, so I just stare at him, locking my hazel eyes with his brown ones, telling him it's not okay. It will never be okay with me. I blame this woman for a lot. It was her; she stole the last of Ty's innocence, practically sold him into the sex trade, and left him with a man whose clients included perverts, kidnappers, and murderers. Frankly, I just want to fucking kill her, or at the very least, beat the ever living crap out of her. I should've kicked her ass in that coffee shop way back when.

"Hey you, what?" I snap when Ty doesn't elaborate.

"I love the shit out of you, okay?"

"Okay?"

"Do me a favor?" He lifts his hands up in a chiming of rainbow bracelets and starts to undo the clasps on the sides of the baby carrier. I watch him, the corner of my lip curling, knowing that Hannah is watching, too. *I want to smash her face in.* "Take Noah for me?" he asks.

"Noah," Hannah says, not like she's asking a question, but

in a creepy way, like she's trying to memorize the information or something. My blood goes cold, even as Ty hands me our son's small, warm, body and looks back over at Hannah from under a loose bit of black hair. He tried to gel it up this morning, but we were in a hurry, so it looks kind of mussy, like he just woke up. I do not like the way that bitch's eyes take this in.

Ty's hands go on his hips and he sucks in a deep breath, running his tongue over his lips and looking devilishly beautiful standing there in scuffed up combat boots and an undone baby carrier, Sharpie bullets stark under the gray light of the morning.

"What the fuck are you doing?" I ask him, noticing that the realtor is creeping back to her. I hope she doesn't call the police. That's the last thing I want to deal with right now.

"Did I ever tell you that I think it's hot as shit when you try to protect me?"

"Did I ever tell you that I don't like being left in the dark? What are you doing?"

"Putting a lid on my past," Ty says, completely ignoring Hannah. To me, she's a threat. To him, she's a piece of his dark, dirty history, a relic best left forgotten. But, obviously, for whatever reason she does not want him to forget her. I can see it written all over her face. I don't know what her deal is, but she still wants Ty for something. Why else would she have written her number on his hand when we saw her in the city? Why else would she have the fucking balls to show up here right now?

Nausea clenches my belly muscles tight, and I think Noah senses my unease because he starts to scream. In the background, Angelica continues to bark, loud shrill yaps that pierce the peaceful silence of the neighborhood.

"I'm sorry," the realtor says, drawing my attention over to

her pinched face, her tiny, round eyes and her mauve lips. "But you'll have to remove the dog before I can show the house." She tries to smile at me, but I can tell she's nervous. She should be. There's violence brewing in the air right now, ready to spew blood across the cracked walls of our collective psyches. One of them is coming down and it isn't going to be mine, and it isn't going to be Ty's. I'll give you one guess.

"Fuck off," I tell her which maybe isn't the best thing to say, but it makes me feel better for a moment, clears my head a little.

"Hannah, let's cut the shit. You didn't come here to look at the house, did you?" Hannah tucks some hair behind her ear and looks over at me, judging me, trying to decide if I really am a threat or not. She has no fucking idea. I've dealt with a lot of shit in my life, and now I have something worth keeping, and nobody is going to screw that up for me. I'm already having to fight with myself, convince my heart that I deserve the husband and the kids and the white fucking picket fence if I want it. It was never in my plans, but now that I've got it, I'm keeping it. This bitch can step off.

"Why else would I come here?" she says, but her voice is so full of bullshit that it stinks. I keep one hand against the back of Noah's head and the other on his lower back, bouncing up and down gently, trying to get him to soothe. He just keeps screaming.

"Might be hungry, Nev," Ty says as I come full circle and give him a look. Ty's staring at me, urging me to go inside, so he can deal with this.

"No," I say. If he thinks I'm leaving him alone with Hannah the Child Fucker, he's gone completely and utterly insane.

"I've got you," he tells me, but I'm afraid that that isn't true, that his demons will eventually drag him to hell if I'm not there for him. He's *always* been there for me. It's my turn again, and I've got to do a good job at it.

Sprinkles of icy rain begin to fall, slapping me on the cheeks and beading on my hair.

"Fuck." I can't stand out here in the rain with a ten week old baby. I just can't and Ty knows it. I start to back away, keeping my gaze focused on the two of them. The realtor blends into the background, becomes just another inanimate object that I have to filter out, so I can see what's going on with the love of my life, my soul mate, my dark horse. When my ankles bump the steps of the front porch, I growl low in my throat and spin around, heading inside and into the kitchen as fast as I can. Noah won't stop crying. He has to be fed. God, but I want to keep my eyes on Ty so bad … Still, I can't make our son suffer for that, now can I? If I did, I'd be as bad as my *mother.*

So I make up a bottle and feed Noah, burp him, and put him to sleep in his crib. The whole time I'm doing this, I don't look out the window. I just do it and I try to enjoy doing it, even though I feel sick, even though I need to know what's going on. I kiss my son on the forehead and run down the stairs, hitting the screen door at the same moment Ty walks in.

He looks up at me, and the expression on his face isn't very pleasant. He's pale and sweaty, and his hands are shaking like crazy.

"What's wrong?" I ask because I know without knowing that something is upsetting Ty. And not just because he's sweating and not because of the glassy sheen in his eyes or the look on his face. I know because Ty and I are two halves of one broken fucking whole, and when we're together I feel complete, and I feel him, and I *am* him somehow because that's the way we were made, me and him. To tell you the truth, I don't think either of us would've survived much longer alone.

I take a step forward.

"She's stalking you?" I ask. Ty bites his lip and glances to the right, over at the vast expanse of living room that our meager furniture doesn't even begin to fill. The corners are dark, filled with shadows. But then, isn't that always the case?

"Something like that," he says, dark hair plastered around the sides of his face, wet from the rain which has just switched from a light sprinkle to a torrential downpour. I rise on the balls of my feet and glance over Ty's muscular shoulder. Both cars are gone.

"What the fuck does that mean?" Ty shakes his head and runs his hands down his face, moving past me to the back door and opening it, so our two stupid pets can come traipsing in, mud trailing in their wake. "Ty?" I can see that he doesn't want to talk about it, not because he wants to keep anything from me necessarily, but because he wants to pretend it never happened. *What did she say to him?*

"Never, I ... " He looks around for a minute, looking panicked. "Where's Noah?"

"He's upstairs," I say, gesturing at the roof with a wild hand. When Ty just stands there and doesn't respond, I move forward and touch my hands to his chest, tangling my fingers in the wet fabric of his red shirt. Whatever it is, we can handle it. I know we can. The one good thing about external tragedy and turmoil is that it prevents you from retreating in, from focusing on all of that internal self-doubt, that bubbling frenzy of tightly clenched pain and the fears and doubts that plague our thoughts like moths. I press a kiss to his wet lips, soft and gentle as a butterfly. His arms come around me fast and hard, squeezing me, smashing me into his chest. "What is it?" I ask, trying to get him to spill before I start imagining worst case scenarios. "What the fuck happened out there?"

"I'm sorry, Never," he says, and he doesn't sound like Ty at all anymore. He sounds like Tyson, the boy who suffered too much, wasn't loved enough. His breathing gets harsh and his whisper tears straight through me. "I'm sorry I fucked up long before I met you, sorry I did things that I regret, that haunt me, that are trying their fucking damnedest to fuck us up." Ty releases me abruptly and turns away, raking his fingers through his hair, closing his eye. "Fuck, fuck, fuck, fuck."

"That's a lot of fucks, even for you McCabe." I put my hands on my hips and try not to panic because that's the first thing I want to do. I want to freak out and start screaming, cussing, shaking him and demanding that he tell me what's going on. But I don't. I hold it all in because he can't, because I'm the other half to to his broken heart, and it's my job to keep this black, bloody thing beating.

He's pacing back and forth, biting at his lip ring, spinning it back and forth with his tongue. That means he's thinking hard about something. But what? What? What? I move forward and grab Ty around the arm, wrapping my hand around his solid bicep, his swarm of butterflies. He pauses then and looks down at me, eyes lost and faraway. I do my best to bring him back, reaching up and grabbing his nose ring, pulling his face down and kissing him again. It seems to work, clears his head just enough that he's able to speak. Demons still dance behind his eyes, but they have no hold over his lips.

"Remember," Ty begins and then has to swallow, run his tongue over his lips. "Remember the story I told? The one about the girl?" I try to smile, but inside, I'm freaking the fuck out.

"I remember all your stories, and I seem to remember there being a lot of girls." I try not to sound jealous when I say this, but I can't help myself. Ty is mine; he's always been mine, even if I didn't know it at the time. I take my eyes from his face and focus on my rings, the red and gold, the silver and blue. Both from Ty, both precious. I lean forward and press my forehead against his skin. "Why?"

"The girl ... the kidnapped one." Ty swallows. His pulse picks up. I can feel it thumping thrumming through his veins. "You remember her, right?"

"How could I ever forget?" That bit of darkness, that horrible sliver of pain is still stuck in Ty's soul, and I don't know how I'm ever going to get it out. I'm going to do my best though, or die trying. Ty swallows and steps back, untangling my hand from his arm, putting his palms on either side of my face. He looks me right in the eyes and lets me see the horror in his gaze.

"Well," he begins, stops, pauses. I have to wonder where this is going, how we got from one house of horrors to the next. This is not about Hannah, not exactly. "People are asking questions, lots of them."

"People?" I ask, trying to puzzle out what's going on. Ty doesn't respond to my question and keeps going.

"And they're starting to get answers. Somehow, someway, these answers are all leading straight to me."

10

Ty is like a rubber ball – he bounces back real quick, even when the odds are stacked against him, even when a lesser man would crumble. Balls to the wall doesn't even begin to describe this man. He's the perfect walking example of perseverance. I wonder absently where he'd be if we hadn't met. Probably in a better place than me. Most likely, I'd still be back at the U, fucking random frat boys and dudes with substance abuse problems. I put a cigarette in my mouth, but don't smoke it, watching as Ty loads up our rental car and tries to figure out how to get the dog crate into the backseat. I figure he'd have been okay. After all, he was the one getting his shit together long before I came into the picture. And it was his idea that we get tested, that we go to SOG. I owe him my fucking soul.

"Holy fuck," he says, stepping back and examining the big plastic rectangle. Angelica watches from a safe distance behind my ankles. As soon as we walked out of the airport, she started to whimper and Ty, softie that he fucking is, let her out. She has no leash. Doesn't need one, I guess. I hold Noah against my chest, tucked safely into his baby carrier, and try to pretend that we didn't get frisked by the TSA for this sole reason, that these delicate bullet drawings played no part. Shit, I'm sure the piercings and the tats had nothing to do with our 'random selection' either.

Ty circles the carrier with his hands on his hips and tries to pretend that he's all cool, super tough shit, that we weren't clutching hands in fearful silence as the plane descended onto the tarmac. *God, I hate fucking flying.* He, like me, has a cig clenched tight between his lips, but it's not lit either. He's promised me that as long as I'm not smoking, neither is he.

"Well, shit," he says, glancing in the backseat of the sedan we've rented and making eyes at the hissing face of Chuck Norris. "We don't really need this damn thing, do we?" I shrug, wondering what it is he's getting at and then watch as he curb stomps the poor kennel with his boots, rendering it to plastic shards right there in the parking lot. Ty grins.

"Aren't you just fucking precious?" I ask, rolling my eyes and doing my best to keep the smile off my face. I don't ever tell him this, but when he does immature shit, I find him cute. *How ridiculous.* "Have fun cleaning that up?"

"Sure you don't want to just jump in the car and drive away?" I give Ty a look and he laughs.

"Okay, okay, I got it," he murmurs around his cigarette. I step back as he bends down and gathers the plastic up, gesturing for the stupid dog to jump into the car and closing the door behind her. I sway on my feet a moment and have to put out a hand to balance against the side of the car. Like a hawk, Ty's eyes snap up to mine. "Are you alright, baby?" I nod and try my best to smile. He knows better, I'm sure, but I'm keeping a game face on for him. Even if I have to retreat to the bathroom every five minutes to puke, I'm going to grin and bear it. For Ty. Always for Ty.

I lean back against the car and let my eyes fluter closed for a moment. I'm exhausted, all the way down to the bone. Last night, Ty and I packed up the rest of our shit. This morning, we got on an airplane. Last night, he confided his fears in me. This morning, he's perfectly fucking fine. I want to talk about it, but I can see that he doesn't. My only hope is that since we're out of New York, his fears are all for naught. He's not wanted for murder or anything, so no detective in his right mind is going to come after him. They might call him, sure, but that's okay. I think that's what he wants. Despite Hannah's warning to the contrary, I think he wants to hell the cops everything he saw all those years ago. If this cold case can get solved, I have a feeling that a little piece of Ty would heal along with it.

Marin Rice.

The girl that Ty saw all those years ago, the one he ran away from but never forgot. The one whose death he blames on himself.

I open my eyes and watch my dark knight gather up the plastic and carry it around the corner in search of a trash can. He thinks I don't know, but I can guess he's going to try and steal a smoke while he's at it. I drop my chin to my chest and look down at Noah, wishing with everything inside of me that he doesn't have to go through the same sort of pain that Ty and I have inside of us. The little monster inside of me, the one that's always told me to do things, who made me into a person I didn't want to be, I have to make sure she's not hereditary. I brush my fingers across Noah's soft tuft of hair.

There's always the chance that Hannah is just stalking Ty, that she didn't come over just to warn him. Why would she anyway? What does she have to gain? Why does she give a fuck? And then again, we don't even know if she's telling the truth or not.

I groan low in my throat and let my head fall back.

Ty believes her. That's what counts. I need to operate off of that assumption.

I pull my lighter out and flip it open, staring down at the flame and salivating at the thought of lighting my cig. An older couple walks by and gives me a pair of looks that could kill. I flip them both off and tuck the lighter back in my pocket. I might've been raised by a white trash mother, but I'm not about to smoke a cigarette with one baby strapped to my chest and another inside my belly. I take my cig out from between my lips and tuck it into my pocket, just in case I need a pacifier later. You never know.

"Back," Ty says, coming around the corner. His unlit cig is still in his mouth. I smile and step forward, running my hand up his chest. He looks down into my eyes and I see an apology burning there. I don't know what it's for or why, but I can see that he means it, genuinely and from the bottom of his heart.

That's when I smell the cigarette smoke.

"Ty," I begin, raising an eyebrow. He laughs, low and deep, masculine and dark. God, I just want to fuck the shit out of him. "That's a bad boy," I whisper, drawing his cigarette from between his lips. I stick it into the left front pocket of his jeans, burying my hand in as deep as I can get it, caressing his leg through the fabric.

"That's right, baby," he says, pressing a chaste kiss to our son's head and then a filthy, immodest one to my lips. "I'm just downright naughty."

We press just a little bit closer, Noah heated between our chests, keeping us apart but pulling us together, yawning like a little butterfly, breath as soft and sweet as the flutter of wings. Ty's tongue teases mine and I heckle him right back, tasting, finding, feeling each other, having a discussion without words. We kiss for what seems like forever, standing there with people staring, wondering who these two young idiots with the weird hair and the tattoos are, why these punks with the baby are lip locked in the middle of the parking lot. What they don't know, but what they should, is that you Never can tell when something is going to go wrong, when life is going to fuck you in all the worst ways. So we take each moment and we treasure it; we take each moment and we stretch it out to forever.

11

I sit in the backseat with Noah and the cat, even though I feel like a tool for doing it. I crawl back there and for the first time ever, kind of, sort of feel like a ... a mom.

"I'm a mom," I tell Ty randomly as we pull out of the parking lot and start down the highway towards my childhood home. "I have a son."

"Well put," Ty says, no sense of mockery in his voice, just a sprinkle of good humor. He tries to look at me in the mirror, but I'm too focused on Noah's face. He's smiling at me and drooling like crazy. I push the end of my sweatshirt up to cover my hand and wipe his chin off with a sleeve covered in bloody skeletons. He doesn't seem to mind so much, blowing happy bubbles when he hears his dad's bangles ringing as he spins the wheel and flips a bitch, turning us back towards the exit we just missed. I have to admit, I'm impressed that he remembers the way. "Don't forget, you're a wife, too."

"Are you trying to piss me off?" I ask, leaning back against the seat and touching Noah's booted feet. Ty's got him dressed in a ridiculous outfit today – well, he dresses him a ridiculous outfit pretty much everyday, but this is the worst – a red and black striped tee with a snarling wolf face on it, a pair of black jeans, and faux combat boots. "Our kid looks like a biker gang reject," I say, noticing for the first time that his pants have fake chains embroidered on the sides. I change my mind; this outfit is probably what got us searched by airport security.

"He's a stud," Ty says, glancing in the rearview again and throwing me a wink. "Just like his daddy."

"I'm dressing him starting tomorrow," I say and when Ty's gaze catches mine for an instant, I can see that innocuous statement means something to him. His smile gets soft, and I have to look away.

"I think he'd love that, Nev."

"I don't think he'll even care," I say, but I glance back over at my baby, *our* baby, and I let him curl his fingers around one of mine.

"Don't say that," Ty whispers, and my heart starts to pump like crazy. My eyelashes drop down to rest on my cheeks and I can feel beads of sweat popping up here and there. I'm really good at the sex stuff and even pretty damn good at the romance stuff, but this … this *family intimacy* thing is killing me. It makes me so uncomfortable that I can't breathe. *I don't deserve this. A broken whore like me doesn't deserve any of this.* My eyes pop open and see that Noah is smiling at me again. I feel ashamed. "He loves you, Nev."

"Ty." Just that one word and he can hear how much I need him, how much I love him. He drapes his right arm over the passenger seat, so I can lean forward and press my face against his skin, hook my fingers around the bronze bangles he's wearing today. I kiss the back of his wrist and close my eyes again, just for a moment, just until I can push this back and focus on more important things. My self-loathing comes last right now. I have to get Ty through this Marin Rice thing, and then I have to decide what to do with … My fingers drop to my belly button, push up the sweatshirt and rest there, feeling, listening to the ebb and flow of my body. Another baby. I'm not even good with the one I have. What if, by bringing in a second, I fuck them both up? What if I've only got enough in me for one?

I bite down on my tongue to push back the panic, turning my head so that my cheek is against Ty's butterflies and my eyes are on Noah.

"I think I might know something that'll make you feel better."

"What's that?"

"I brought the strawberry flavored lube in my carry-on, just in case you wanted to give me a blow job while I'm driving." I sit up and stare at the back of his head.

"You're kidding me, right?" Ty chuckles.

"Of course I am," he says, but I'm not sure that he is. Still, I roll my eyes and feel relief in my annoyance. Ty knows me too well. "Oh, and check this out." He gestures absently with his right hand. "Look in the side pocket of Noah's baby bag. I bought you guys a joint gift." I raise my eyebrows and bend down, dragging the bag across the floor and between my feet. I dive in and search around, pushing past diapers, wipes, a pack of Marlboros (what kind of parents are we?), and some extra socks. And then I find it.

"This is the most atrocious thing I've ever seen," I tell him and he grins. "What the fuck even is this?"

"It's a pirate hat. For Noah."

"This is dumb," I say, but I'm smiling. Always smiling when it comes to Ty fucking McCabe.

"Ah," he says, snapping his fingers like he's just remembered something. "I forgot. Check in the pocket again. I'm pretty sure it came with an eye patch."

I love that fucking man.

12

"Why is your baby dressed like Long John Silver?" This comes from Beth, is, in fact, the first thing that comes out of her mouth when we climb out of the car and unhook Noah from his car seat. Ty laughs hysterically, and I have to pause for a moment and take in the sound, like embers falling from the night sky. Beautiful, strong, clear. It's probably the nicest laugh I have ever heard come out of that boy's mouth.

Beth has a baby carrier strapped to her chest, but unlike ours, it has no bullets on it. Not half as cool. When we make eye contact, our hazel eyes reflecting one another like a mirror, she starts to cry. Her hot, fat tears fall on her daughter's head as she holds out her hands and touches the sides of my face.

Beth looks tired, worn-out, like maybe there's something going on that she's not telling me.

"Are you alright?" I ask as she tries to kiss my cheek. I pull back and give her a look. Her hair is longer and a little disheveled. The perfect bob cut she had last Christmas has not been properly taken care of. I guess I don't really blame her. If I didn't have a baby daddy like Ty, I doubt I'd even get the chance to shower, let alone have my hair done. I wonder what Danny 'The Douche' Delphino's done this time.

"I'm just happy to see you," she says, turning from me and focusing her attention on Noah. I realize that this is the first time she's ever seen him in person. More tears fall on poor Autumn's head. I haven't met her yet, but I already know what she looks like: copper colored hair starting to peek in, hazel eyes, pale skin and pink cheeks. I would've known that without even looking at the hordes of pictures Beth always sends. Except for poor Noah, the entire family is made up of copper haired clones, father's lineage aside. Only Ty's genes were strong enough to break the pattern. I find myself scoping his ass out and busy myself by getting out a cigarette.

Beth reaches back and slaps it to the ground without even looking my way.

"God," she says, touching my son's cheeks, making kissy-faces at him. "He's even cuter in real life." She pauses. "Except for the whole pirate thing." Ty laughs again, but Beth ignores him. She lets him get away with murder. "Noah," she coos. "Meet your cousin, Autumn. Want to say hi?" Beth lets Noah wrap his fingers around one of hers and makes a little waving motion.

Ty looks at me over her head and tosses me a self-assured

smile. I'm not sure what it's for, but it's sexy as hell. My mind wanders to the tractor in the backyard …

"This is going to be great," Beth says, watching as I move around to open the trunk on the car. "Having the kids grow up together. I always wanted the girls to feel what it was like having a big family."

"Enormous," I say, but Beth isn't really listening.

"Maybe if we can scrape up the money, we could do an extension or something, make things a little more comfortable, a little more permanent." I give her a look, leaning around the trunk, so she can see how serious I am right now.

"This is not permanent. This is in-between, Beth."

She opens her mouth to speak when a car sounds on the driveway behind us. I don't even need to turn around to know who it is. *Noah Scott.* I swallow hard and spin.

Bitch-Never has her head sticking out the front window, tongue lolling. Angelica, who has yet to jump out of the back seat, perks up and starts barking, voice loud and gruff in the still air. Both babies start to cry.

"Want me to take him inside?" Ty says, but I know what he's really asking. *Do you need a moment alone with Noah?* The fact that he's even willing to give me that means everything. Ty trusts me not to do anything stupid, and I appreciate that, I really do. I turn to look at him, holding our baby in his arms, ringed fingers wrapped around his midsection. They look so damn cute together. I nod, reaching out to lay my finger's on Autumn's chubby shoulder. Beth smiles.

"He called and asked if he could come over." She shrugs and starts to move away, following after Ty.

"Beth?" I ask, and she pauses to look at me. "Did Zella and Noah ever … did anything ever happen between them?" If it did, Zella won't talk about it, and she answers all my questions about Noah with vague, broad-brush bullshit. Beth just shakes her head.

"I don't know," she answers honestly. "Why?"

"No reason," I tell her aloud, but inside, there is a reason. I feel responsible for Noah's broken heart, like I snapped it in two and gave one half to Ty. I want him to be happy and somehow, in some weird way, I feel like if he gets with Zella, he'll be a part of my family, and that's something I've always dreamed of in one way or another. I wonder if Ty suspects any of this.

The sleek, black sedan pulls up next to me with a purr. I reach out a hand to pet Bitch-Never and she bites me, straight up. I slap her in the muzzle and step back with a sigh.

"Fucking cunt," I growl as I use my leg to keep Angelica from jumping all over Noah Scott's very pristine, very expensive whatever-the-fuck-it-is.

"Never!" I hear Noah yelling from inside the cab. The dog retreats inside the vehicle and proceeds to railroad her supposed master, stomping his crotch and exploding out into into the fields around the house. Angelica follows, and I let her go, confident that if I called, she'd come back. Noah emerges next, a little disheveled, an awful lot cute. I smile at him.

"That dog is almost as ornery as me," I say, wondering what he thinks about me naming my son after him. I try to decide if I should let him bring it up or if I should take the initiative.

Noah pauses, blonde hair shifting in the breeze, blue eyes twinkling, and he smiles at me, letting it all out, not holding anything back. His white T-shirt sticks to his body and emphasizes a few changes – since we left, Noah Scott's gotten *buff*.

"Never," he says, slamming his door, watching me watch

him. He's absorbing me, appreciating me, but he isn't going to try, not anymore. I know that, and it makes me happy and sad both. Happy because I know he's accepted that Ty and I can never be separated, not without a massive hemorrhage of love and darkness that would kill us both. But also sad because it means he's a great fucking guy who deserves better than I gave him. *Goddamn it, Zella, make your fucking move!* I vow to call and bitch at her later tonight. "I missed you like crazy," he says and then he comes over and gives me a hug. It's not as awkward as I thought. Noah feels good, like a friend I've had forever. Maybe not my best friend because that spot is and always Ty McCabe's, but maybe a close second or something, right up there with Lacey Setter who I haven't seen in for-fucking-ever. He pulls back and glances over at the house. Ty is nowhere to be seen. *He isn't even spying on us? Is this man for real?* "Is little Noah around?" he asks, turning back to me with a grin. "God, I can't even believe you named him after me. I'm honored, I ... " Noah pauses and digs around in the back pocket of his designer jeans, the ones that only further emphasize that metrosexual look he has going on. "I wrote a poem."

I laugh and take out the piece of paper he's extended to me. Noah takes a deep breath in and then lets it out.

"How was New York these last few months?" he asks as my eyes scan the words, absorb the beauty layered in them with awe. Noah Scott is so fucking talented at this shit. If there was any market for poetry, he'd be a millionaire.

Clandestine beauty revealed in time's extent, born of moths and butterflies./Hearts of broken now repaired, connected first with sanctity and oft forgotten truth./And all the strings that severed, tied together, broken never.

I fold the page back up and put it in my sweater pocket.

"It was ... a rainbow," I tell him and he cocks a golden

brow. "And I don't mean that it was all sugarplums and kittens, just that it was all different colors. It was good, bad, just everything." I think for a minute and decide to add something, just in case he got the wrong idea. "I wouldn't have changed it for the world." Noah smiles softly. "You ready to meet your namesake?" I ask and he grins.

"I'm actually dying to see him, Never. I always thought you'd make beautiful babies." I smile back at him, but mine is tinged with sadness. He seems okay, but I can hear the meaning in poor Noah Scott's message. *I always thought we'd make beautiful babies.* I think he had always planned on marrying me and having a family. When that didn't work out, I guess he just didn't know what to do. He still wants that, but he just doesn't know who to want it with.

13

Inside, the house is chaos. There are Regali women everywhere, cooing over babies, picking at the holes in Ty's pants, screaming. It is absolutely *insane*.

Noah and I weave our way into the mess and wade through copper haired hugs and hazel eyed gazes, cheek kisses and teary blubbering. Ty is waiting for us, leaning up against the door frame in the kitchen, watching India cradle his baby and smiling about it. When he sees me, he scoops me up under the ass and Frenches the ever living shit out of me. I feel his erection through his pants when he presses me close, but it's hardly the time to enjoy it. I'm forced to pretend it's not there when what I really want to do is grab that strawberry lube and suck his fucking cock. My eyelashes flutter a bit as he sits me down, and I feel a wave of dizziness sweep over me. *So he is jealous of Noah Scott,* I think as Ty looks down at me with a smoldering gaze, cutting straight through to my core, burning me alive in the best sense possible. I look up into his face and smirk. A jealous Ty is a sexy fucking Ty. I might have to egg him on a bit.

I turn back to the kitchen mob and realize that I've forgotten about Noah. He's already managed to find his way over to the baby and has him in his arms. Behind me, Ty crosses his arms over his chest and bristles a bit, but he says nothing.

"Having man instinct problems?" I whisper to him as the chaos swirls around us.

"Just a little," he says, and I can hear the hint of a laugh in his voice. "The rival male is holding my cub, you know, so I gotta be a little pissed. Anything else would just be unnatural, right?" He drapes his arms around my neck and soaks me with his heat, his smell, drenches me with that dark edge that cuts just right. I shiver.

"I'm making mutton for dinner tonight," Beth says, and there's a very audible groan that sounds from the room.

"Mutton?" Jade asks from her position near the back door. She's regarding Mini McCabe like he's the strangest creature she's ever seen while simultaneously scowling. Her copper hair is pulled back into a high ponytail and her cheeks are painted an obnoxious red, making her look like she's fucking around for Halloween instead of doing her best to accent her cheeks. I don't much like the snakeskin mini she's wearing either, but I guess I have no room to talk: the T-shirt I'm wearing under my sweater has a zombie baby on it. To each her own though I kind of think my sister looks like a whore. *Maybe it's a good thing you're here. I think she needs you.* "What the fuck is that?"

"Baa," Lorri imitates before Beth tosses her a *look.* She shuts up.

"You don't like your nephew?" I ask when Jade continues to stare, arms crossed tight over her chest, lips pursed. She shrugs.

"I just can't believe that *you* of all people gave birth to a child. It seems ... unnatural." She shrugs again. I pull a magnet off the fridge and throw it at her. She steps out of the way and then gives me the finger. "I'm going to go downtown for a little while," she tells Beth. Immediately, my oldest sister goes from nurturing and motherly to dragon-esque in her rage. I wonder if I'll ever be like that, if I'll ever throw Noah looks tough enough to kill. It's hard to imagine at this point.

"No, you are not," she says, as if Jade is sixteen, not twenty-one. "I told you, when you get a job you can – "

"I already have a fucking job," she snarls back. Beth's face gets real nasty then, proving that she is a Regali sister at heart. We all have a little dark blood in us. Fortunately, it hasn't rotted our souls from the inside out like it's done to Angelica, but it's there, will always be there. We just have to learn to live with it.

"Five hours a week at a coffee shop doesn't cut it. When you're earning enough to pay your portion of the bills, then you can go out and drink your ass off. I don't care. But until then, don't bring it up again. You're not blowing all your money on alcohol, so you can hang out with your deadbeat drunkard sperm donor!" Beth's voice rises with each word until she's practically screaming. She jerks the oven open and the smell wafts out, hitting me like a truck, making me double over with nausea. Ty grabs onto my arm and helps keep me on my feet. "And stop using the freaking F-bomb around the kids."

I glance up from under my dark hair and see Jade looking back at me, tears in her eyes, her lip quivering. Then she turns and runs out of the house. I don't hear her car start, so I have no idea where she goes, but at least it isn't into town.

She's seeing him.

The man that killed my father.

That tried to rape her.

How? Why?

I'm having a really hard fucking time coming to terms with that.

"I gotta use the toilet," I cough out, stumbling into the bathroom and folding myself just in time for the puke. If anything, it seems like this pregnancy is going to be even *worse* than the last. If I carry it to term. If. If. If. Shit.

Ty follows me in and I get this terrible sense of déjà vu, like we've been here, done this. But I have to remember that we're stronger now, better. I can deal with this. *We* will deal with this.

"Do you want to talk about it?"

"What is there to say?" I ask as I spit into the murky water and flush it down. I rise to my feet and turn on the faucet, scooping cool liquid into my mouth and gurgling gently. I spit again and wipe my sweatshirt sleeve across my lips. When I glance up into the mirror, I look young, too young to be a mother. My face is soft and my eyes are hard. I question my own strength and then glance away. "If Jade wants to see that piece of shit, what can I do to stop her? I might ask her why, but that's all I can do. I doubt she'll even answer me."

Ty doesn't say anything, but he reaches out and brushes my hair back with his rings, all twelve of them, glittering and sparkling like rubies. They match the piercings in his face. Gotta love a color coordinated badass.

Neither of us misses how small and tight this bathroom is, how close we are, how hard he was in the kitchen.

"Ty," I warn as he comes up behind me and slides his fingers under my shirt, up my belly, cupping my tender breasts with strong hands. "So not fair," I groan, reaching up and smacking the fan. It coughs to life and is loud as fuck, blocking any sounds from escaping this little room. "You can't touch those." My cunt is pulsing and my heart is pounding in my skull. Down below, I know I'm soaking wet.

"Why not?" he whispers against my ear. "It'll make you feel better."

"It'll make *you* feel better," I tell him, but he's already unzipping his pants and pushing my sweats down. The fabric doesn't resist, just falls straight to the floor in a pool, leaving me bare and ready to get fucked by my baby's father. *God, that turns me on. I feel so fucking stupid, but Jesus ... no wonder I'm knocked up again.*

"It's not good for pregnant mommies to be stressed, Nev. You have to take good care of yourself and stay calm. If this is what I have to do, I'm prepared to make sacrifices, baby. And don't even fucking *think* of trying to thank me for it." Ty dives into me with a grunt, pushing himself in as far as he can go, thrusting hard and fast. With my cheek pressed against the mirror and my hands splayed out on the tile countertop, I almost feel like I'm back in college with one of the naughty boys from the parties, one of the ones who wear black and smoke like chimneys. One of the ones like Ty McCabe.

This reminds me of my dirty past, but it isn't my dirty past, this is my new future and the man behind me is a fucking god, and I'm his goddamn goddess, so it doesn't matter if we're rutting like alley cats in a half bath. It's perfect. It's absolutely fucking perfect.

I groan low and loud, and only Ty's ringed hand clamping over my mouth stops me from screaming as he pounds my ass with his hips and spills himself inside of me. About a second later, my orgasm hits and I collapse into his arms with his breath against my neck and his warm body against my back. All around us, the darkness settles and bursts into vibrant, brilliant light.

14

Angelica Regali comes home later that evening and pauses in the doorway to the living room.

"Where's the baby?" she asks me, purse hanging from one hand, menthol cigarette clutched in the other. Darla gets up from the couch, wiggling out from beneath my arm and runs over to her, throwing her arms around my mother's bare legs, clinging to the willowy skirt she's got on. Angelica sets her purse down and runs her fingers through her youngest daughter's hair.

"He's sleeping up in Beth's room until the crib gets here," I tell her, honestly baffled that she even gives a shit. "Did you … did you want to see him?" Ty's hand squeezes my waist hard. I think he can tell I need the support right now. *You're cutting her off, remember? What she says, what she does, they have no bearing on you and your soul.* Still, I don't think anybody misses how needy my voice sounds when I ask that question.

"Don't wake him up now or he'll get to screaming," Angelica says, which is much more in character for her. Darla is talking to her now, telling her all sorts of useless things about the day, useless things that my mother should be clinging onto with her every breath, listening intently to, caring about with every bit of her soul. Because that's what mothers are supposed to do. I think. *See, Never, it isn't so hard. You can do this. You know you can.* "But in the morning," she continues, bending down and giving my little sister a very, very rare hug. "I'd like to." And then she's sticking her cig in her mouth and disappearing up the stairs.

Darla watches her go and waves bye, retreating back into the living room and the empty couch cushion on my right. India exchanges a glance with me from across the room. She's sitting on the other sofa with Noah Scott on her right and Lettie on her left. Everybody else is either in bed or MIA. Jade hasn't come home since the kitchen incident, the one that very nearly turned into a walk of shame. If Beth hadn't caught the oven on fire at the exact moment Ty and I were fucking, somebody would've known. In this house, somebody *always* knows.

"Is Lorri upset about having to share a room again?" I ask. Must suck to move into your own room and then get kicked right back out. I feel like such a failure. My heart starts to flutter, and I begin to worry if leaving New York really was the right idea or not.

"She's okay," India says with a shrug. But then she smiles at me. "I think she's just glad that you're back, permanently. We all are."

"Why does everybody keep saying that," I groan, letting my head fall back onto the couch cushion. It feels so damn good ... I start to drift off immediately. "This is only temporary until we decide what our next step is."

"Doesn't matter. We're just happy you're here," India says, and I hear the couch creaking. I open my eyes and lift my head up.

"I should probably get going," Noah says, rubbing his palms together. "I've got class pretty early in the morning." He smiles. "Finals are coming up next week, so I can't miss a thing." I look at him with a bit of nostalgia. School sounds fucking great right now. I just want to learn shit. I don't even care what it is that I'm learning. My mind wants to grow so big that I just fucking explodes with all the knowledge I'm cramming into it. "Maybe we could make Christmas plans or something?" he says. "I know Zella wanted to do something big this year. I told her you're all welcome to use the cabin at the lake." I watch his face for signs. When he says my sister's name, it flows off his lips like a promise. *Zel-la.* I wonder if he realizes that. I return his smile with a smirk.

He doesn't get it. Poor, innocent, little Noah, the antonym of Tyson Monroe.

"Cabin, huh?" Ty asks, rubbing at the piercing in his eyebrow. "Is this one of those rich people cabins with a hundred rooms or some shit?" Noah flushes a light pink color. It looks good on him.

"Well, a dozen rooms," he says which sounds so ridiculous that even I laugh. "And an anatomically correct deer statue in the front entryway. It's little vulgar." Ty chuckles and stands up in a clattering of bracelets. He stretches his arms over his head and holds out his hand for Noah to shake, pulling him into one of those man hug things where they punch each other on the back. Seeing them together makes me feel good inside, whole, like I'm come full circle and completed my journey. It's not true, of course. Our journeys never end, and there is no such thing as happily ever after. It's happily for now or happily ever sometimes because there are always rough patches. The best thing we can do is ride them out and take one on the chin. For now though, the boy I loved and the man I love are hugging and calling each other *dude*, so I'm happy. In this exact moment in time, I am fucking ecstatic.

"Thanks for loaning us your name, man," Ty says as he and Noah separate. They smile at one another just as I'm blindsided by a big double dose of baby revenge: nausea and extreme horniness. At the same time. Great.

Noah moves over to say goodbye to me, but I bolt right past him and into the downstairs bathroom. India follows this time, not Ty and stands in the doorway with a quizzical look. She doesn't know that I'm pregnant again, nobody does but Beth. Just Beth, the mom I always wanted and never knew I had.

"Are you okay?" she asks, reaching out a hand and then dropping it back by her side. "Should I get you some Pepto or something?" I shake my head and try to keep the next wave down. I ate Beth's mutton. That was a big fucking mistake. "Are you sure?" Another head shake. India doesn't know that these Mini McCabe babies are badass. They don't want pink goopy medicine; they want to announce their presence to the world and stomp all over it.

"No, I'm good," I tell her, holding back another gag. She looks down at me with her gorgeous face, a face that's free of pain and strife. It's good to see that, to know that not everybody in this godforsaken world is totally fucked. My little sister has a chance to be happy, to really truly find that fucking nugget of good in the world and consume it whole, without taking a dose of anguish to wash it down with. I pray to whatever deities will listen to someone as fucked up as me that she finds what Ty and I have, gets it without paying her dues first. "Will you get Ty for me?"

She steps backwards into the hall and cranes her neck up the stairs.

"He's putting Darla to bed," she tells me which makes me smile, just a little. For doing his best to integrate into my screwed up mess of a family, Ty deserves a Purple Heart or some shit.

I groan as I force myself to my feet and slump against the counter. I am exhausted. Last night, I got absolutely zero sleep, and it wasn't Noah's fault. It was Hannah's. Ty tossed and turned and groaned in his sleep, face twisted with pain and guilt. Why did she have to seek him out and tell him that. *Marin's family has gotten desperate. After all these years, they've finally scraped together a reward worthy of conning even the filthiest souls in the city. They know he saw her. They know he saw who she was with. They know; they know; they know. And they're coming.*

I snap to with India's hands grabbing me under the arms as I slump to the floor.

"Never!" she screams which is a little overdramatic but understandable. I don't know what happened, but I was blacking out I suppose. Stress. Fatigue. Flying. Dark souled babies. It could happen to anyone.

"I'm okay," I tell her as heavy footsteps slam down the stairs and Tyson fucking McCabe comes leaping over the banister like a superhero. Or a villain. Either or. He stumbles into the bathroom, nearly tripping over the laces he never ties. His shaking hands grab my face on either side as he unintentionally crowding my sister out in his worry.

"What happened?" he asks me, completely and utterly serious, terrified even. I look into his eyes and I can see how much I mean to him. It brings tears to my own and sends India scurrying away without another word.

"Stop looking at me like that," I tell him, trying to push him away. Ty refuses to let go.

"Never, I heard India scream bloody murder. Something happened. I'm not letting go until you tell me what." I grab onto his wrists and look up, down, around, anywhere but as his face. I'm not going to cry again. I am sick and fucking tired of sobbing like a whiny baby. Almost a year to the day we stood in this same house with this same problem. I survived it then, and I'm in a better place now. Why is this still so hard? Why am I still making stupid decisions and thinking stupid thoughts and acting like a goddamn bitch? Oh, that's right. Because I'm an ex sex addict with mommy issues and a daddy that's six feet under. I have issues. Fine. We all get that. But can we move on? Can *I* move on for Christ's sake?

"You're an asshole," I tell him firmly. There's no brooking argument with this voice. Ty doesn't even try.

"No, I'm a man that hearts the fuck out of his wife, who worries about her day in and day out, who thinks about her every waking moment every sleeping one, too. I'm a dad that loves his kid and wants to make sure he sees what a freaking awesome person his mother is. I'm a guy that's never loved anything or anyone half as much as I love you."

"Ty." That one word, a whisper, a promise. My arms go around his neck, his lips find my throat, and then he's pressing me up against the wall and my body is screaming for it. *Lacey would love to hear about this shit.* "Fuck me," I beg him.

"No." I give him a look that's akin to sheer horror.

"What?"

"Not until you tell me what happened." I roll my eyes and push him away. He lets me go this time and scoots back, so I can step out of the bathroom, putting my hands on my hips and taking long, deep breaths. I don't want Ty to think I'm giving in for sex. If he doesn't want to sleep with me, he can watch while I masturbate on the floor of our bedroom, dressed only in one of his T-shirts. Let's see how long he can resist that for.

But I did promise to be honest with him, so I'm going to, no matter what.

"I blacked out. Sort of. Just for a second. India caught me as I was falling." I shrug. Ty narrows his eyes on me.

"Are you okay?"

"I'm pregnant."

"Never ... " I take that cigarette out of my pocket and run it under my nose.

"I'll keep you posted," I tell him, putting it between my lips and moving out the front door to stand on the porch. Ty follows and promptly plucks it from my mouth, putting it up to his and lighting the end.

"No direct smoking. You can live vicariously through me."

"Secondhand smoke kills, McCabe."

"So does a whole lot of other stuff. Tell me about this black out." I roll my eyes.

"I lost consciousness for a split second. I didn't even know it was happening until it was over. I feel fine. I'm tired, a little dizzy, nauseous and horny as hell. Basically, I'm infected with your seed again." Ty blows smoke out of his nostrils, and I have to look away because it makes me want to jump his ass right then and there. I figure he's going to keep teasing me, so I sit down on the porch swing and wait. When the barbs don't come, I look up at him and see that he looks miserable, stretched thin. It only lasts for a second and then he's blinking it away, focusing on me and running his tongue across his lips.

"Never, I can't wait anymore," he tells me as I look up at him, confused. "I want to make a decision. No, I *need* to. Are we keeping this baby?"

The question surprises me although it shouldn't, really. This is an important decision, something I don't take lightly, but that needs to be made. Last time, it wasn't really much of a choice at all. In my heart, I knew all along. Just like I do now. I might be insecure and a little damaged, but if you give me some time, I get it. Eventually, I figure it out. I look down at the dirty fabric of the swing and start to pick at the fraying fibers with my fingernail.

"Why?" I ask him. "I mean why right now, why this second?"

"Because I love you more than fucking anything, and if it comes down to you or her, it's always going to be you." Ty gestures angrily with his cigarette and then falls down to his knee in front of me, leaning his forehead against the front of my legs. I tangle my fingers up in his hair and inhale deep, tasting smoke and the promise of rain, the whisper of snow. It's like last year all over again, but this time, I'm better prepared, this time I'm stronger and I'm ready to fight harder. If I'm so worried about not being worthy, then I have to prove myself. I have to become worthy and validate myself in my own eyes. I know that in Ty's, I'm already perfect.

"How do you know it's a her?" I ask softly, noticing that our dog is sitting on the foot of the steps looking up at us, eyes brown but wise, like she knows a whole fuckload more about this earth than I do. I don't doubt that for a second.

"Because our son is a freak in the Regali family line, the only boy, the only one without copper hair." Ty taps my flat belly with his knuckles. "If we don't have a copper clone in there, I'll be surprised." Ty pauses and inhales sharply. "If you think you can do this, if you want to do this, know that I'm right there with you." Ty doesn't say it so many words, but I know he wants this baby, that he'll want all our babies because each one is a symbol, a physical manifestation of *us*. I swallow and try to speak as Ty adjusts himself, filling the ear the sound of bells as his bracelets hum down his arm and clank against the bars of the swing. He looks up at me and waits patiently, his young face pretty and perfect, his eyes filled with old soul.

"You … " I start to speak, and I choke. I try to talk, and I stumble. Ty is there to catch me, always and forever.

"I promise not to put an eye patch on her," he says, completely and totally serious.

"Are you sure you want to make that promise?" I ask him, also serious. "Because I don't know if it's one you're necessarily going to be able to keep." Ty smiles and he knows without hearing my answer that he's won.

"I get to see you all cute and preggers again?"

"Ty … " I begin as he takes my hand in his and kisses my wedding ring with ardent fire raging through his mouth and infecting me through the skin, heating me up to my boiling point and right over the edge. I have to hold back a gasp and a wave of dizziness.

"Never."

"Ty."

"See a doctor for me?"

"McCabe, I think you'd know by now. I'd do anything for you."

15

It's no secret that after highs, come lows, that after hills, come valleys, so it shouldn't surprise me when I wake up early the next morning with shaking hands and fearful thoughts. I imagine giving birth to a daughter, one with hazel eyes and copper hair, and I imagine her hating me with every ounce of herself the way I hate my mother. I imagine Ty becoming disgusted with me when he sees what a horrible person I am, when my true colors come out around my kids and I fuck it. Fortunately, I make it into the bathroom and switch on the shower before I start sobbing. Off I go again, crying even though I shouldn't, acting like a little bitch when I should be strong for Ty. I sit there on the tiles with warm water streaming down the sides of my face, soaking my pajamas and dragging me down in folds of heavy fabric.

When I finally pull myself far enough out of my slump to get undressed, I find red in my underwear. White splotches cover my vision and I slump back against the wall. *What is this? What's wrong with me?* I stare at the fabric for so long that the shower watches most of the stain away and leaves me wondering if I imagined it all along.

I bite my lip and toss the panties out with the rest of the clothes, grabbing my shampoo and scrubbing at my scalp like I've got a bone to pick with it. I scrape my skin with my nails, and the pain feels good, makes me feel better for a brief moment, long enough that I can pull my emotions together and get control over myself. I touch a hand to my stomach, drop it down low, feel around my vagina, teasing, probing. Everything was fine last night when Ty and I made love. Everything felt okay, but … I don't know what to do. Tell Ty should be the obvious choice, but then I wonder again if I'm just imagining it. The panties look clean now, and I have been a little off lately. It can't have been as bad as I thought. It was just some spotting. I tell myself to woman up and get over it. Being pregnant is like earning a badge of courage or some shit. It separates the girls from the women.

By the time Ty climbs in beside me, I'm feeling better, but I don't want to lie. Out of fucking everything that's happened, I know that's one sacred bond I won't break. So I tell him about it and he looks sick to his freaking stomach. I promise him I'll go to the doctor at some point in the not too far off future and change the subject, but the fear is still etched around his mouth.

I watch it follow him out of the shower, into a black T-shirt with and jeans, a pair of brown boots. I watch it chase him as he switches out his facial piercings for silver studs. I watch it harangue him while he moves down the stairs and into the living room, searching for his son.

"Hey Mini McCabe," he says as he takes the baby from India and gives him a kiss on the head. I pause at the bottom of the stairs and feel suddenly shy, like I don't know what to do with these two men. Ty and me alone is okay, but with the baby, I just … I'm not good at family dynamics. I love my sisters, but I've been out of the loop for so long. Ty just stands there and stares at me. "You okay?" he asks, concern lacing his voice. I nod and try to smile, but it doesn't reach my eyes and he can tell. He tries to hand me the baby, but I don't hold out my arms and instead cross them over my chest.

You are a mom, Never. This is your son. This is your baby. Kiss him and hold and let him know that you love him more than you love yourself, that you wouldn't trade him for anything in this world, that you care.

I find myself frozen, embarrassed, ashamed. Ty takes the baby back and presses him into his chest, tilting his head to the side and examining me like he isn't quite sure what to make of this.

"Nev, he wants to see you," Ty tells me, and I almost breakthrough the storm cloud that's hanging over my head, shirk off the dark for a brief moment, and step forward. But then I see Angelica, and I just go blank. The bitch will always affect me, no matter what I think. I've cut her off, but the emotional ties I had to sever still bleed every now and again.

"Can I see him?" she asks, fairly unceremoniously. Ty looks at her and then back at me, asking what he should do with his eyes. "Hello?" Angelica asks, getting annoyed. Ty waits for another second, but when I don't respond, he spins the baby around and lets my mother look. Just look. Maybe touch. But not hold. Not without my expression permission. Angelica purses her pretty lips and adjusts a copper curl that's fallen into her face. "I'd like to hold my grandson."

"You forgot your daughter's birthday," Ty responds, not at all apologetic about it. He's pissed, and he isn't even talking about me. He's talking about Darla. Beth planned a huge party for her last month, decorated the whole house, even convinced Ty and me to get on Skype and participate. She told my mom a hundred times; my sisters told her a thousand; Darla a million.

She didn't show up.

"It was a mistake," Angelica grounds out between her teeth. They used to be pretty and straight, but now they're starting to yellow, and they look crooked to me. I could be imagining it, but maybe not.

"It was a date," Ty says with a shrug. "You can say hi to my kid, but you're not holding him. You haven't earned that right."

"I raised eight fucking kids in this house, and now you're telling me that I'm not qualified to hold a damn baby?"

"I'm telling you that you haven't earned the privilege." My mother scoffs.

"Now it's a privilege to hold your little brat? Fuck you. I want you out of my house." Ty gives her a look that says *I'm not going fucking anywhere.* He doesn't even have to say anything. Ty McCabe communicates with his body as much as his voice. He's so animated and passionate and just … God, he's too good for me. Really. He is. "You better be gone by the time I get back," she snarls, shoving past him, not caring that he's holding my infant.

Darkness descends on me, violent and tumultuous. I want to sob, but I also want to kill her. *Stupid hormones.* I turn away and try to take shallow breaths, so I can get a hold of myself. When I look back, Ty is staring at me.

"Never," he says softly. "It's okay. You are not her. You will *never* be her."

I don't know what to say, how to respond to that and tell him my fears, let them spill from me like a tsunami and overtake us both. I open my mouth once and snap it shut. When my phone rings, I answer it. Ty looks disappointed which makes my stomach drop, but I have to deal with these issues on my own. I can't burden him with anymore darkness. We're both finally crawling out of the cave and into the light. He might be a few feet ahead of me, but if I dump this on him, I could leave him behind. I won't do that.

"Never?"

It's Lacey.

"Hey," I answer, glad for the reprieve. Ty raises his eyebrows and moves away, giving us some privacy. "How's it going?" I miss my roommate sometimes. I mean, I was never really that good to her when I was there, but she was my only friend. I shiver a little. Just thinking of what it was like, alone and desperate, grasping straws in my quest to find something worth living for, dreading weekends because I was most suicidal then. I bite my lip so hard it bleeds.

"Okay, I guess. We have finals next week, so you know, *ugh.* What are you up to?" I lick the blood away and decide to test my news on Lacey before I use it on the rest of my family. Beth seemed okay with it, but you never know how the others might react, and I don't want to do anything to disappoint them, to make them doubt me. I just want to be loved by them.

"Um, guess what?" I ask her, and she gets all excited. Being around Lacey is like being around a cocker spaniel or something. I can already imagine her tail wagging happily at the thought of good gossip. "I'm pregnant again."

"Shut the fuck up!" she says, and I think I hear giggling in the background. Trini, I assume. The two of them are inseparable now. Lacey keeps saying they're going to run away to Massachusetts and get married, but who the fuck knows? "That was quick. I didn't even know you *could* get pregnant that soon after giving birth."

"Yeah, neither did I." I sit down on the bottom step and sigh heavily. "But yeah, I guess it's possible."

"Without condoms, it's not just possible but probable," Lacey says and I narrow my eyes. She thinks it's funny because her partner can't knock her up if she tried. Mine can impregnate me with a single kiss, a glance, the touch of his hand across mine. *Fucking stud.*

"Thanks for the education," I say. "I sure hope you're using dental dams." Lacey doesn't take offense to this. In fact, she really doesn't take offense to much of anything. She's so … light. It's nice to see there really are people like that in the world, that not everybody has to be dragging around enough baggage to sink an ocean liner. That gives me hope for my sisters, my son, my … whoever it is that's inside of me now. I feel a little flicker of proud for saving Lacey at the convenience store. If she'd gotten raped, a little monster might've climbed into her heart and darkened the skies around her. This, of course, makes me think about Ty and how we met, really met, how we picked me up out of the glass and carried me outside, pulled shards from my skin, and sat on the beach with me to talk. Just talk. About nothing and everything, open and honest. I hope to God I don't screw things up with him.

"I was calling to see what you're doing for Christmas," she says, and I can already tell that she has something in mind.

"Apparently, we're going to my ex-boyfriend's cabin

wherein lies an anatomically correct statue of a buck and the opportunity to convince my younger sister to bite the bullet and try to get in his pants." Lacey laughs, but only because she isn't looking Noah Scott in the face in one of those epic *oops* moments that haunt you for life. "Shit."

He pauses awkwardly by the door, but it's too late for either of us to pretend he hasn't heard. We both stay very, very still.

"I want to see you, and we don't have any plans, and I really, really need to see little Noah, so … "

"I'll text you the address here," I say and she squeals. My eyes are still locked onto the baby blues of the man I lost it to, who was so sweet and kind, who I totally and completely fucked over. What if, somehow, I damage Ty the way I damaged Noah? What if I'm just not meant to be with any one person? Maybe that's why I slept around so much … because I'm not worthy of keeping. I shake my head to clear it of this bullshit. "I'll send over our schedule when we know what it is."

"Yay! Okay, love you, Nev. I'll talk to you later. Trini and I are about to hit up the beach." The phone call ends and I drop it into my lap. I clear my throat and get ready to apologize but Noah interrupts me.

"We had a one-night stand, Never."

"Yeah, I mean, I guess you could call it that," I say, feeling offended that that's how he remembers us. It might've been one night, but it wasn't a stand, it was a declaration. I pined for him for years, and that's how he thinks of us? Noah lifts up his hands and looks back and forth, flicking his eyes here and there like he expects Ty to jump out and growl. And you know, he just might do that.

"Not you and me, Zella and me." My brows climb high and kiss my scalp. Nausea climbs my throat when a meaty smell wafts out of the kitchen, but I push it back. Noah sighs and leans against the wall, closing his eyes and sucking in a humongous breath.

"When?" I need to know everything, all the details. This is such bull. That little bitch has been keeping secrets from me. I wonder what else Zella is up to back in Texas.

"The day you left to go to New York. I, we, I knew for sure we were done for good, and I just … I lost it. I cried and I … I broke a window in your bedroom." I think about it, but can't picture anything different. I must not have been paying attention. Either that or the midwestern wind has already coated the window is so much dirt and gunk that it doesn't look new anymore.

"Why?" Now it's my turn to look around and see if Ty's listening in. But my reasons are different than Noah's. I *want* Ty to hear. I want him to know the pain I inflicted on another person. I want him to know he can't trust me. But most of all, I want him to sweep back in here and take me in his arms. God, I'm fucking needy.

"I loved you so much," Noah says, keeping his eyes closed, doing his best to control his breathing. "I waited for you for so long, and then not to even have a chance … " He finally drops his chin and cracks his gaze, focusing all of that longing and need into a single beam. I have to glance away because it's not right for me to accept this. I have no hold on him, and he will never have a hold on me. I've got to convince him to move on. I thought he was okay, but this look, these feelings. Maybe he's not? "Zella was there, and we'd been talking for years, so … we had sex." He swallows hard. "And I told her I wasn't interested in a relationship. I mean, I told her that before we had sex, so she'd know. I wasn't over you yet."

"Have you talked about this with her?" Noah shakes his head.

"After we … finished, she got up and left. It was like you

all over again. She went back to fucking Texas." He sounds exasperated, tired, worn out. I feel sorry him, and guiltier than ever. "I wrote her a really nasty email and then, I don't know. She won't talk to me anymore." I blink at him slowly, trying to come to terms with this. Noah Scott made a mistake. Noah Scott is capable of making mistakes. Noah Scott is not perfect. Huh. "I want to apologize, Never. I want to see her again. But I … she sent me that note about the cabin, but it was clinical. She wasn't really talking to me. She was just asking to use my place." I cock my head to the side and automatically go for a cigarette. Gossip and smokes are like cheese and wine, they just fucking go together. Plus, I'm liking this. Noah is getting further and further away from boyfriend and lover status and closer to friend, cementing himself into that space where I always knew he'd be. Now to figure out this little dilemma. I try not to admit it to myself, but I like drama when it isn't related to me. I mean, not directly. The baby and the mom thing and Hannah … those things are my problem. This is just far enough away from my black soul that I can get into it and be helpful. I think.

"She knows that you'll be there, Noah," I say, thinking of my sister. There's a five year gap in our relationship, sure, but I'd like to think I know enough about her to predict her behavior. "She asked because she wants to see you." He doesn't look like he believes me. I watch as he runs his hand though his blonde hair. His buff new body is starting to make sense … "Are you interested in her?" He stares at me, and I can see in his eyes that he doesn't want to answer the question.

"I've only ever slept with two women," he says, and I see where this is going.

"Me and Zella?" Noah shrugs. "Shit." He licks his lips and lowers his voice. His hands are trembling a bit, whether from adrenaline or fear, I'm not sure. "Well, that's good I guess. If everybody has their hands in the pie, it probably doesn't taste as good." I sound so bitter when I say this that Noah takes a step back like he's been slapped. I don't mean to inject any of my pain into this, but I can't help it. It's been surfacing a lot lately. I blame the baby again, the one in my belly.

"Can I ask you a question?" he begins, and I'm already nodding, chewing on the end of my cig and praying that there was some way I could actually smoke it. I take it between two fingers and slide it out. Just the motion feels fucking good.

"Sure."

"Do you think my inexperience had anything to do with the situation?" He's dead serious when he asks this question, and it's about now that McCabe's sharp laugh echoes out from the kitchen. We both turn to look and see him sliding out from the space beside the refrigerator, emerging from the shadows all dark and liquid, sexy as hell, smoldering, like a damn flame lighting me up from the inside out. I have to pause and catch my breath.

"Sorry," he says, and when he sees me looking at him, he smirks. "I was trying to be polite and stay out of it, but I felt like I needed to step in."

"Step off, McCabe," I say to him as he takes in the cigarette with a raised brow. "Where's my fucking baby?"

"Your fucking baby is with your fucking sister in the fucking yard." He smiles and I throw my cig at him. Miraculously, he catches it between two fingers, glances around to see if Beth's watching and lights up. He's going to get himself into serious trouble. She might be being nice to him right now, but once he gets on her bad side, he's in tough shit. I'm not bailing him out. My sister is far too imposing for that. "Did she come?"

"Ty," I groan, but he isn't listening. He's just changed from my soulmate, my dark, twisted other half, the black to my berry, the beat to my drums, the blood to my brain, and turned into a guy. And not just any type of guy, a slutty, pervy whore of a guy, a bad boy extraordinaire, dolling out sex advice to the less fortunate.

"She ... " Noah looks at me, like maybe he's not sure if he should continue or not. There's no way in shit I'm leaving them to have *bro time*, so I stay put and glare.

"I have a lot of experience," I say purposely, making Ty bristle. He grits his teeth and blows smoke out his nostrils. It tangles around his nose ring and teases the air with the sweet, sweet scent of tobacco. "So go ahead. Not that I think that matters. This isn't inexperience or over experience or just being a downright fucking slut." Noah looks confused, but Ty looks *hungry.* I lick my lips and Noah takes another step back from the two of us, eyeing us warily. "Zella is fucking *obsessed* with you and you hurt her. You have to make it up to her somehow. If you want to, that is. You never answered my question: are you interested in her?"

"I think I might love her," he blurts. Ty raises his brows and puffs out his lower lip.

"You hear that, baby, he might love her." He looks back at me, and I can see that he's boiling over with jealousy. We've both fucked our fair share of people, but I'm the only one who ever had sex with someone I cared about. He hates that. It drives him nuts.

I rise to my feet.

"Might is a strong word, Noah. It also means there's a possibility that you don't. Figure it out first, and then talk to her. She'll know. Women always know." I turn around and start up the stairs, trailing a wave of dark smoke in my wake. Ty follows it, just like I wanted him to, accosts me at the top of the stairs and slams me into the wall. "This is spousal abuse," I tell him, but down there, I'm soaking wet.

"You were begging for it, baby," he grounds out around his cigarette. I forget all about the weirdness of Angelica and the pregnancy and my inadequacy as a mother, and I just get lost in Ty. Besides, a good fuck never hurt to fill that empty hole inside. And if Ty's the one that's filling it, all the better.

"Actually, I was just coming up here to grab a book. I'm not interested in you right now."

"Your kitty cat's telling me otherwise," he purrs, still not playing husband or father or soul mate, still playing bad boy.

"I can't believe you just said that," I murmur as his hand travels down the front of my pants and teases my clit through the hideous cotton granny panties I'm wearing. "Why are you so antsy all of a sudden. Does it bother you when I talk about all the guys I've fucked?" Ty growls, low and deep, takes a deep breath and tries to pull himself out of it.

"No, baby, I've accepted it. Soon, you'll be swollen with our second child, ripe with my fucking seed." Okay, maybe not. He's still deep down in there, buried in darkness, but the good kind now, not the painful kind. "Does it bother you that I've fucked lots of women?"

"You're a slut," I whisper as he licks my ear and spins me around.

"You're a skank," he says with a delicious half grin.

"Whore."

"Cunt." He bites the word off with his teeth, so that it lands in the air like a compliment. He steps back suddenly and grabs me by the hand, dragging me into our bedroom and tossing his cig into an ashtray. There's not much in here now – boxes, an air mattress, our suitcases. This doesn't stop him from getting what he wants. He grabs the waistband of my pants and drops to the floor, dragging them down, exposing the copper curls between my legs. He presses his face there and breathes deep, flicking his eyes up to my face. I stare down at him defiantly as he untangles the pants from my ankles and stands back up.

Ty grabs me under the ass and lifts me up. My legs go around him and my mouth drops to his, singeing and scorching, devouring. His cock teases me, kisses my opening, and forces its way in, claiming, marking, taking me. I snag his hair in my fingers, squeeze it tight, owning him right back.

"You're mine," I whisper, breathless, full, smoldering with heat.

"Right back at ya, baby," he snarls, fucking me so hard and fast that I can feel friction burning between our pelvises, rocking me right over the precipice of pleasure and onto that dangerous line where pain sits crouched, watching from the other side.

I try to come up with a smart-ass retort, something to sting his ego and get a rise out of him, but I just can't seem to think in English anymore. My words are gone. I exist in sound and touch and kiss and fuck. I become that moment, wrapped up in Ty, full with him, squeezing him as tight as I can, worshipping him while he worships me.

A dark goddess meets her dark god, and the storm she thought was brewing over her head transforms into the dancing shadows cast by the light, not bad but different. Different, belonging solely to her, only to her.

Ty comes inside of me; I come all over him. It's disgusting, messy and perfect. Just too goddamn perfect. As I pant in his arms and feel his body pressing into mine, I worry about one thing and one thing only: perfection is a passing quality, so how, how, how can this possibly last?

16

Beth invites me to this 'mommy and me' picnic thing for women with children under the age of two. She says it's mostly there, so we can sit around and gossip, fill up in good southern barbeque.

The very idea of it scares the shit out of me.

I don't tell anyone this, but being alone with Noah frightens me. What if something happens? What if he starts choking? What if wails in public and I can't get him to stop? There are so many things that could go wrong that when I imagine being with the baby without Ty's help, I get jittery and my hands start to shake.

I don't know how to explain this to Beth though, and end up getting enrolled in it anyway. When Ty hears about it, he's pretty fucking ecstatic which makes me feel so guilty, I want to crawl under a rock and die.

"That'll be so great, babe," he says, holding me, snuggling me. It feels so *damn* good. I can't even believe I spent the majority of my life avoiding this part of intimacy. Sex is great, but this ... This completes the act. Yeah, I'm a complete girl, so what? Cuddling is underappreciated. "You and Mini never get to spend any time alone together. How is he supposed to grow up to be a mama's boy if you guys don't hang out together?"

And how am I supposed to say no to that?

So, the next fucking morning starts off with Beth trying to help me pick out an outfit (I refused), India trying to get me to take one of Beth's six floral patterned baby carriers (I choose my own, Sharpie bullets and all), and Ty trying to dress our kid in a Sasquatch outfit (not fucking happening).

"What the fuck is this?" I ask, pointing at the furry lump in the crib. The poor baby looks like he's been dipped in a vat of dirty dog hair. I push the hood off his head and stare at the costume. It's ... well, there aren't really any words for it in the English language. I try though, goddamn it, I try real, real hard. "This is sixty shades of what the fucked up. Take it off."

"What are you talking about?" Ty asks, snapping photos with his phone. He holds up his ringed hand and waves at the baby. Noah coos and kicks his legs in response. When I try to smile at him, he just drools. "He looks fucking precious as shit. You'll be the envy of all the other moms." Ty grins. "Especially when your hunky husband shows up midway through and takes you in the bathroom for some alone time." I let out a harsh bark of a laugh and clamp my hand over my mouth. Noah gurgles excitedly.

"You do realize that after this one is birthed, you're never getting laid again. I'm becoming celibate. Enjoy your last few months of sex."

"Hey, Never," Ty says, getting serious all of a sudden. It scares me a little when he gets like this, demons dancing behind his eyes, howling for escape. "Sex means nothing if it's not with you." I look at him, and I have no clue what to say. Fortunately, Beth comes into her room and sees us staring into the crib Noah shares with Autumn.

"What did you do to that poor baby?" she asks, leaning down and squinting. "Jesus, Never." I roll my eyes and watch as she moves away, shaking her head. "I have plenty of gender neutral one pieces … "

"It's fine, Beth," I say as I touch my finger to the sole of my son's foot. My son. *Son.* I'm going to have to go in the bathroom at some point and lock the door, stare into the mirror and say that a hundred times fast. Son. Son. Son. Son. Son.

"Yeah, don't worry, Beth," Ty says smiling softly at me. "I won't pick anymore outfits out for the kid. Never's going to start taking care of that." He raises a brow at me, challenging my earlier words. I swallow hard.

"Yeah, I got this," I say as Ty moves away, leaving me alone with the baby and a dirty diaper. Now, listen up and listen good: I have only changed about a dozen diapers since Noah came home from the hospital. All of them were filled with piss. This one, on the other hand … All I know is that Ty is too good to me. I'm becoming spoiled, like some sort of rotten piece of fruit, filled with maggots, surrounded by fruit flies. I'm despicable. I take a deep breath and almost call out to my sister when she leaves, footsteps disappearing down the hallway.

I look down at Noah and wrap my arms across my chest.

"Hey," I say. The baby gurgles. "Um, I want you to know something." He drools on his chin and stares at me like I'm the most interesting thing he's ever seen. His lips twitch in a smile. My eyes can't hold his. They're like mirrors to my own, grey with blue and green flecks. He might have McCabe's dark hair, but there's still some Regali in there somewhere. "I love you," I say and the words catch in my throat, strange and foreign, choking me with tears and making it hard for me to breathe. "But I don't know how to be a mom. I'm trying, but I'm scared. Do you know what I mean?" Noah moves his arms around, looking ridiculous in that stupid Sasquatch suit. I take a step forward and wipe my hand across my nose, trying not to sniffle. I'm being ridiculous. Absolutely ridiculous. I've been through way tougher shit than this. This is nothing. This is love. It's that simple.

I reach down and pull his furry pants off, tossing them into the hamper. Our conversation comes to a bit of a halt as I gag and do my best to clean up my son. When I'm finished, and he's dressed only in a clean diaper, I continue. He can't understand me, but maybe he'll absorb some of the feelings I'm trying to portray.

"Mommy," I say and then wrinkle my nose. Okay, fuck that. I am not a mommy. I can be a mom and a mother and a mama, but not a *mommy*. "Mom doesn't ... she's had kind of a shitty life, and it's not your fault, it's just that I ... I want to do right by you and I don't know how." I start wrangling Noah into a black tee with a ghostly silhouette on the front. "Little goth baby," I say which strikes me as funny. I start to life and end up crying again. Noah takes this all in stride, listening to his mother's sob story with a smile. "She lost her dad at a really young age and uh, it was fucking horrible." I get the shirt on and move onto the pants. Little jeans slip over his chubby legs as I get into the groove of this. "And then she hurt her friend so bad, he's having trouble moving on to other women." I pause. Frown. "Just because you're Ty's son doesn't mean you can be a player, okay? You have to treat women with respect." Noah drools a little. I wipe it away with my university sweater, the one that says *We don't give a dam about your team!* "This next part gets kind of X-rated, so I'm going to simplify it a little. I … looked for love in all the wrong places, forgot who I really was inside and almost lost my soul." This is the worst part of the story, but I'm smiling the widest now because this is where everything changed. This is where two tortured souls found each other in a bar and clashed, came together in a random twist of fate, united as one and did amazing fucking things together. "But I've got it back now, I think, or at least I'm on the right path." I slip socks and shoes on my son's feet and pick him up, breathe him in, hold him tight. "I'm going to go back to school and learn something random like … Japanese. And then I'm going to take my degree and write a book about broken girls with desperate souls, and then … who the fuck knows, kid. With your dad and me, anything is possible."

The floorboards in the hallway creek, and my head snaps up. I move over to the door and kick it open only to find McCabe standing there with his hands over his face. He spreads his ringed fingers and looks out at me. My mouth drops open, and I think seriously about hitting him.

"I didn't meant to eavesdrop," he whispers, dropping his hands altogether. His face is so solid right now, dead serious and full of a tender love that makes my lip tremble and my eyes seek everything but him. "I thought you might need help with the baby. I was going to leave when you started talking, but, fuck, Never. You're so damn incredible."

"That was a private conversation, Ty," I whisper. I want to start a fight, but I can't. Not with all of these feelings floating around between us.

"I know, and I'm sorry, baby." He tries to smile, but ends up laughing instead. He runs his hands down his face again. The butterflies on his arms wink at me.

"Thanks," I tell him randomly, and he glances at me with a raised brow.

"For?"

"For giving me your jacket that day, for taking me to that clinic, for following me to the bus station. Basically, thanks for not giving up on me." I step forward and kiss him on the cheek. "I have a stupid housewife gala to attend. See you later."

As I start to walk away, Ty reaches out and grabs me, surrounding Noah and me with a swarm of colorful butterflies, breathing into my hair and sighing deep.

"Thanks for not letting go of me when I fucked up, for forgiving me when I was an ass, for being the most, beautiful goddamn woman I have ever seen."

"Ty, stop," I say, as the darkness teases me and the little monster commands me to tell him off. *You are not good enough, will Never be good enough. You are a useless, washed up whore with no future. Fuck you, Never. Fuck you forever.* I squeeze my eyes shut tight and then snap them open, pushing back, fighting against the dark cloud, telling the little monster to go suck dick.

And it works. For the moment, it works and I feel better. The blackness recedes, like the tide pulling out from the shore. It doesn't go very far, but I watch it's descent, and I wonder. If I keep fighting, if I stay strong, will it leave me forever? Will it pull so far back that it's nothing but a glimmer in the distance? It's definitely worth a fucking try.

"Never?" Ty asks, sensing something in me. I lean my head into him and smile, feeling just a little better, a little freer.

Until the drama starts downstairs. And then I think about nothing because I can hear Beth screaming from the living room. I glance back at Ty, and he explodes into action, taking the stairs two at a time. I follow after him, keeping the baby's head tucked safely against my chest. When I hit the bottom floor, the voices become clear and my lip curls.

Danny.

Shit.

"My fucktard-dar is going crazy right now," Ty tells me as he watches the explosion unfolding before him. I think we both thought, with the commotion and all, that Danny had hit Beth. Not yet. But things are going from bad to worse, so who knows. I love Ty even more for the fact that he's willing to defend my sister.

"We have plans, Daniel," she screeches, voice pitched to a level I've only ever heard a sprinkling of times. One of which was right before I left, before she betrayed me in the worst way possible, chose a murderer over her own sister. *No. No. I can't think like that. It's over and done and we are past that shit.*

"The court doesn't care if you have plans, Beth. I get the kids half the time. Check the papers."

"You can burn in hell," she snarls, tucking some hair behind her. The short bits promptly escape and get stuck to her sweaty forehead. "You only come over here for two things: to fuck me or to piss me off. Well, I'm done with fucking you, so the only real reason you're here is to ruin my damn day. Come back tomorrow, Danny." I watch the exchange, taking in *Daniel's* pale, lifeless eyes and his big, square teeth. He's like a Ken doll gone wrong, like if Ken had been dipped in a vat of dickwad-psycho-sack. I glare at him, but I don't interfere. Not yet. Watching this man in his expensive suit and his greased up hair, I have a hard time understanding how Beth has not one but *two* children by this man. It's just … unfathomable. I guess I can't judge her. Like me, Beth has had some problems with men (thanks, Mom!), she just made the mistake of getting pregnant with one of her screwups. Twice. It kind of makes my head hurt.

"I guarantee if you send me away without my daughters, you'll regret it." Danny picks up Autumn's car seat without waiting for answer from my sister. She clenches her fists, but doesn't move, just stands there with Maple on the floor behind her, scooting blocks around the carpet. She's so wrapped up in that douche bag that she's forgotten her no cussing rule. I look at my sister standing there, face pale and sweaty, eyes wide and brimming with tears. I look at Danny taking Autumn's blanket off and tossing it to the floor like he can't even bear the sight of such a filthy thing.

I turn to Ty and hand him Noah. He takes the baby without thinking about it because, well, that's just what Ty fucking does.

"You're the world's hottest motherfucking daddy," I tell him, biting his ear and spinning on my heel, moving into the living room and taking the car seat by the handle. Danny is so surprised to see me there that he doesn't protest.

"Don't make a scene," I say quietly, dangerously. I have a lot of rage inside, a big ol' pot of it that I used to take out on the people around me. Considering those people have been pretty damn good to me lately, the pot is now full. Hannah is damn lucky that Ty stepped in. "Just go and come back tomorrow. It really isn't that difficult to comprehend."

"Give me back my daughter," Danny grinds out between his thick teeth.

"Never," Beth says.

"Hey, asshole," says Ty. "If you touch my pregnant wife, I will fucking kill you and dump your body in the Mississippi." I don't need Ty to defend me, but I like it anyway, so I don't say anything, just stand there and smile. Danny looks at Beth, at Maple, at Ty with an infant clutched in his strong arms, his gently curving sweeps of bicep that can rock a baby to sleep and give a man a concussion just as easily.

"Next time you think you're helping your sister," he says, and in his eyes I know he's remembering last year, the engagement ring, the fight with Ty. "You may want to consider the consequences." Danny wipes his hand across his jaw and shakes his head, storming out the door and cringing with Angelica growls at him from her spot on the porch swing.

We all stand quietly while he goes, waiting until we hear the car start.

"Thanks," Beth says, but she just sounds tired, and I think I can finally peg the worry in her voice, the fear hiding behind her eyes. She flops onto the couch and puts her fingers to her forehead. Maple crawls into her lap and snuggles her belly. I watch her carefully, wishing she had a partner like Ty, someone who made things better and not worse.

I bring Autumn's car seat over to her side of the living room and set it down gently.

"You okay?" I ask her, but she doesn't respond. "You want me to kill him?" It's a joke. Sort of. Beth doesn't smile.

"I'm just tired, Never," she whispers. "And I don't want to go to the picnic anymore. You can go without me if you'd like." *Fat chance that's happening.* I step back and glance over at Ty who's fuming a little, bristling with aggression. I look back at Beth.

"If you need anything," I tell her, reaching out and brushing some hair from her forehead. "Come find me, okay?" She nods but doesn't say anything else. I move out of the living room and take Ty with me to the den to check on Chuck Norris. He is not enjoying his two weeks of indoor time, and has taken to pissing all over the bathroom floor. Ty won't let me clean that up either, but I try.

"What the fuck was that about?" Ty whispers as I open the door and use my foot to keep a hissing Chuck back. "There was something going on there we weren't getting."

"Yeah," I say as Ty slips inside and closes the door. Looks like Mr. Norris has been using his litter box, but he's taken to scratching up the old couch. There are shreds of fabric hanging like torn flesh. The cat takes a swipe at me and then immediately goes and rubs on the holey legs of Ty's jeans. "Something that I know is just going to spiral out of fucking control." When I said I liked drama, I meant the more passive type. Not things like this, things that threaten my sister-mother's happiness, that hurt her children. I narrow my eyes. "Are we the only people in this house who aren't falling apart?"

"Love is glue, baby," Ty says, but his voice isn't at all playful, only serious now. "Without it, sometimes the cracks begin to show."

17

When our stuff finally arrives from New York, I get a wave of nostalgia for the shitty, old house and the silence that permeated the shabby rooms, the way they were only filled with sound when the two of us were in them. I love my sisters, but shit. I guess I forgot what it was like to live with them.

"Screw you, you fucking bitch!" Jade screeches at Beth. They're having another fight. Over what, I'm not sure, but I don't care. Right now, I'm lying on the couch while Ty unloads the truck with the movers, directing them to put the extra items in the barn and the rest in our room. I move the washcloth off of my eyes and watch as they drag Noah's crib up the stairs. Tonight's going to be his first night back in the room with Ty and me. I enjoyed the baby free nights for sure, but I'm kind of ... glad he's going to be with us. For now anyway. Soon as he's old enough to start recognizing when Ty and I are fucking, he's getting his own room. "This shit is so old, Beth. I don't want to talk about it anymore." Jade storms past the living room, copper hair flowing out behind her. She pauses for a moment and meets my eyes.

I stare straight back at her and dare her to come in and talk to me. She looks away quickly and disappears up the stairs. I haven't asked her about Luis. Frankly, I have enough shit to deal with right now. And anyway, talking to Jade when she isn't ready to talk about something usually results in a scene similar to the one I just witnessed. I don't have the energy to deal with that crap. I feel like complete shit again, brought to my knees by Ty's baby. I hate this feeling of weakness, but there's not a damn thing I can do about it. Sometime in the next few days, I'm guessing that Ty's going to drag me to a doctor, so I can have my legs propped up like an extra in a BDSM film, strapped down to a sterile table with a spotlight on my damn crotch. I shiver. I don't even know if I want to go to a hospital this time. I'd rather birth the kid by myself.

I lean my head back against the couch and end up falling asleep without knowing it. My eyes close and all of a sudden, time just passes me by, sucked away from me without my permission.

When I wake up, the sunshine is long gone and the house is dark. There's a blanket over me and a dog lying across my legs. I struggle to sit up and try to figure out what's so strange about this moment.

Silence.

The house is quiet. For the first time since I moved back in, it's completely still in here.

I kick Angelica off and stand up, stretching and rubbing at my head. I feel groggy, but better. With a yawn, I move out of the living room and into the kitchen where my butterfly bad boy is sitting hunched over a computer, eyes droopy, bracelets jingling as he navigates around a familiar blue and yellow website.

"Hey," I whisper, and he jumps, turning to face me with a slight smile.

"Hey," he says and he scoots his chair back, so I can sit in his lap. Ty's body is solid and warm behind me, a granite pillar of independence and strength, perseverance and trust. I can't even imagine how I ever survived without him. He's the other half of my soul, the love of my life, the one person who could match me, blood for blood, pain for pain. But I also know that I have to get control of myself to make this happen. I'm working on it, and I'm getting better, but I'm not perfect. There are still things that can set me off. My best hope is to avoid them completely until I'm ready. Unfortunately, sometimes those sorts of things are just out of your control.

"What are you up to?" I ask, and I hear the grin in Ty's voice before I see it.

"Ordering your transcripts." I wrinkle my brow.

"Why?"

"We're enrolling you in school, Never." I turn all the way around, so that I'm facing Ty and not the computer, tangling my fingers together behind his neck.

"We are?" His grin just gets bigger.

"I know you wanted to go back, so I thought you could continue here, locally. Just for a little while, until you decide where you want to go and what you want to do." I frown at him.

"But what about you?" I ask as he pulls me closer, breathing hot against my neck, nipping at the soft flesh with his teeth. The metal of his lip ring presses into my throat and makes me gasp.

"Aw, fuck, Nev, do you think I'd let you go to school without me? Hang out at all the frat parties with your plump, pregnant little ass peeking out from under a miniskirt?"

"Um, please," I say, trying to pretend that his mouth on my skin doesn't affect me at all. There's no denying that I've cast a spell on him though. His magic fucking wand is stabbing me in the right thigh. "I'm a senior, McCabe. You're a freshman. There's no way in shit we'd be hanging out together." Ty makes a pretend moue of disappointment. And then he tries to feel up my tits. I slap his hand away. "Be serious for a second."

His face drops and he takes a massive inhale of winter air. Outside the house, the first flakes of snow begin to fall, drifting like ballerinas, pirouetting across the harsh Midwestern earth and turning it soft. Blurring the edges of reality. Shifting perception by altering the landscape. It's all false, a nice blanket, something that covers up the wounds of the land, hides them until it's too late, until all the snow is melted and the damage is done. Trading wintery kisses for the burn of frostbite.

"Nev, I want to counsel kids. I want to prevent more people from becoming like you and me." He pauses, gestures with his ringed hand. "Well, the way we used to be anyway. I think it's possible to have what we have now without needing to suffer for it first."

"I agree."

Ty pauses and spins his lip ring around with his tongue.

"Nev?" Just my name, serious, too serious. My heart

starts to pound.

"Don't, Ty," I tell him, afraid that he's going to say something that'll break my heart and split me into a million, jagged pieces. I can't have that. I need him. I need him here with me forever. I push my forehead into his. "You can't talk about our future and then use a tone like that. I said get serious, not fucking morbid."

"Never, I want to talk to the police."

Shit. Damn. Fuck. Not this again. I don't want this in our life. I just want it to go away, sweep it under the rug with all of the other crap that happened in the past, pour gasoline on the fibers and let it rip.

"It happened a decade ago, Ty, a lifetime ago."

"It haunts me every fucking day."

"You didn't do anything."

"That's right. I didn't."

I look into Ty's face. He wants to tell the police what he saw all those years ago, tell them about poor Marin Rice, the girl he didn't hurt but didn't save either. Ty wants to be a good man. It doesn't take an expert to dig deep into his damaged psyche to figure that one out. He's desperate for it; it shows in his eyes each and every time his gaze wanders to the horizon. What he doesn't realize is that he's already a good man, that in my eyes, he's the perfect man. This old wound of his is still bleeding, gushing blood, spraying it across his eyes and blinding him.

"What if they decide you're a suspect?"

"They won't." He pauses, rubs at his chin. "At least I don't fucking think so."

"What if Hannah was lying, Ty? What if she was blowing smoke up your ass?" Already, he's shaking his head.

"Hannah is … fucked up. I don't know what her problem is or why she came to me, but I don't give a shit. This isn't about her, babe. I looked it up online. I saw it. They reopened the case, and the Rice family really is offering a reward." I swallow hard and pat my pockets down for a cigarette. I don't have any. I got rid of them all this morning, dumped them into the garbage can and watched as India dragged it down to the street for pickup. I'm no good with temptation. I let my eyes flutter closed and try my best not to think about how my lips are tingling and my hands are shaking. I want to tilt my head up and blow smoke at the ceiling, breathe deep and taste nicotine in my lungs.

"Did you even know the couple she was with? This is stupid, Ty. You can't help her. She's dead." I look him straight in the face and try not to get angry. He can't risk everything we've built up for *this*. His past and mine put together aren't worth a fucking cent, let alone a life.

"She's dead because of me, Never," he snaps, and I realize that that's the first time he's gotten angry with me since we moved into his grandma's house. "I am fucking responsible for this shit. It hangs on me everyday and weighs me down. I have to get it off my shoulders or I'm going to fucking drown."

"You don't have to redeem yourself," I scream at him, pushing him away, standing up, spinning. "Remember? What happened to what you said before? That only Noah and I mattered. What about that, Ty?"

"Never," he says, and his voice gets soft again. He tries to come to me, but I back away, putting my hands up and shaking my head.

"You said nothing else mattered. So fuck this girl. Fuck her. Fuck Marin Rice."

"Nev, calm down," Ty says, hands up placatingly. "Baby, come here. Just come here."

"No," I growl at him, ready to fight him to the death on this. "I won't let you get involved in this. You said yourself that the sex trade has its own set of rules. If you break them, what happens then, Ty? Even if the police believe you, or you call in anonymously, somebody will know, won't they?"

"It's not a yakuza clan, Nev." He tries to smile, but he doesn't look happy. There are no dimples there. "It'll probably end up being nothing, a fifteen fucking minute phone conversation that the police will document and forget all about."

"Then why?" I ask, and I feel like crying, but I don't. Like I said, I have a lot of rage inside. Ty doesn't deserve to have any of it directed his way, but there it is. I can't help it. It just comes out, and I regret it the moment it does. *This isn't us anymore. Ty and I are past this. We don't need this drama. All we need is each other.* "So you can tell the police that some freaking nut job named 'Dick Prick' fucked you over? Sent you into the pits of hell and then died before he could pay up for crimes committed?" I make little quotes with my fingers when I say what dead fuck's name. I wish he were still alive, so I could hunt him down and destroy.

If Ty was unhappy before, he looks *really* ticked off now. He digs into his back pocket and, despite our promise to quit, ends up with a cigarette in his shaking hands which he lights and takes a drag on, right there in front of me. Teasing me. Screwing around with my nicotine addiction and making a cranky prego bitch absolutely insane.

"So they can write down the stupidest fucking monicker ever known to man and laugh about it?" I don't mean this as an insult to Ty, more in that I don't believe the police are worth shit when it comes down to it. None of them were there to help Ty when he needed them most, and that is their job, isn't it? Where were *they* when Marin Rice was still alive? Where were they when Ty and his cousin were suffering?

But this offends Ty, fucking rips into him and sends him

over the edge. Maybe we both needed one last freak-out, one last chance to express some of this pain and rid ourselves of it forever, bleed it dry and let it shrivel up to die in the sun, just the way it deserves. Either that or we're just experiencing human error, that essential erring we all have that comes out very now and again. It happens to all of us; it's just the best of us that learn to triumph over it.

"That man with the fucking laughable name made me suck his dick, Never. He raped my goddamn mouth, and he enjoyed it. I don't think it's all that fucking funny." I stare into Ty's brown eyes, watch the gray smoke curl up and kiss his dark hair. I could tell him then that I don't mean it that way, that I'm sorry, and he'd probably forgive me, but I don't. I just stand there and watch the cherry crackle in the dark stillness of the house, the only figure right now who's glowing with anything akin to cheer. Ty lets it dangle from his lips and smashes the top down on the laptop, turning around and flicking off the kitchen light, throwing us into complete darkness. I watch the orange dot of fire as he spins around. "And it's not okay, and I'm not really over it, and I don't know if I'll ever be over it. Do you think I like kissing you with this filthy mouth? Do you think I like kissing our goddamn son?"

Again, perfect opportunity for me to say something like, *I happen to enjoy your filthy mouth.* But I don't. A part of me thinks that I want this fight, want my little monster to be proven right, want to be shown that perfection does not last, and Ty and I are not a fairytale couple.

He steps forward, but all I can see is the shadow of him, the silhouette. The rest of Ty McCabe is shrouded in darkness. The cigarette moves, lighting up the kitchen like a firefly as Ty pulls it from his lips. He blows smoke out and it kisses my forehead like a butterfly's wings, soft and so insignificant that it becomes significant, like it's the most important sensation in the world.

"I want to call the police, and I want to tell them my name, and I want to give them every detail I ever learned about anyone ever involved in that shit. I want to tell them about Hannah before she starts fucking stalking me, and I want to tell them about Dick and how he really screwed with my head, and I want to tell them about Marin Rice, the girl that torments my fucking soul. Maybe then I'll feel alright, like I'm a little cleaner, a pound lighter, and I'll feel like I deserve you."

"Deserve me?" I ask and even the whisper that escapes my dry lips feel like a curse. Tears are rolling down my cheeks again, bleeding sorrow for Ty McCabe and his pain. *How can he even say that? I'm the one that doesn't deserve him, the one who fucked not to survive but to cope, who couldn't even handle her own feelings. This is the same girl that stands before him now, unsure how to respond to life like a normal person, screwing each thing up as she goes, bleeding darkness across a blue, blue sky.* "Ty McCabe, you deserve a woman twice as good as me."

The cigarette flops, falls to the floor. I think it burns the linoleum, but neither of us is really paying attention to it.

"Never, that's a goddamn lie. There isn't a single, fucking woman on this earth that even holds a candle to the beauty I see in you."

"I don't deserve you." There. It's out. Ty stays silent for a moment.

"You don't," he says, and I almost pass out, hit the floor and never wake up, a Sleeping Beauty with no prince, a Cinderella without a ball, a woman who turns back into a whore at the stroke of midnight. "You deserve far better than some crusty old cum dumpster."

"Tyson Monroe McCabe," I snap, using his full name for God only knows the fuck why. Is it a mom thing? I figure it must be. "Don't you ever fucking talk about yourself like that again, or I swear, I will kill you where you stand. You're *perfect*. Doting husband, nurturing father, spewing wise wizard shit wherever you go."

"Wise wizard?" he asks, the hint of a laugh in his voice. "What the fuck does that mean?" I lean back against the sink and look up at the ceiling, buried in shadows above us. It seems to go on forever from where I stand, but I guess it's just more proof that the darkness has to end somewhere, that there's always a limit.

"It means you say shit that makes sense, only you do it by dropping the F-bomb every six seconds." I lick my lips, taste the salty tears on my cheeks. "I never say anything worth repeating, Ty. I'm just a broken girl with a shitty mother who's afraid of her own baby." Ty takes a step forward, but I keep talking, letting the tornado of self-doubt bullshit I have inside of me out. That doesn't mean it's gone or that I'm cured, but it'll help, and at least I can feel better knowing that Ty knows it's there, that he knows the awful truth about me.

"You're afraid of the baby?" he asks, and his voice is much softer now. "Why?"

"Everything I touch turns to shit," I tell him. "And I'm afraid. I'm afraid I'll ruin him, that I'll turn into Angelica somehow." Ty moves forward, and I scoot away, around the table, so he can't touch me. "And it's worse than that even. I don't … I don't know how to hold him or how to feel about him or … " I lick my lips. "I don't feel like a mom. I don't even feel like a woman. I don't deserve you or Noah or," I flick my finger against my stomach. "Whoever this is."

"Mrs. McCabe," Ty says, and I can tell he's trying to get me to lighten up. "Come here."

"No." I move around to the other side of the table and look defiantly at the darkness where his face should be. I drum my fingers on the table. Silence descends. And then, tricky little fuck that he is, Ty is vaulting over the tabletop and landing next to me, grabbing me by the shoulders and kissing the shit out of me, pushing me back, slamming us into the wall. "Ty, stop," I say, but I don't struggle very hard. Why should? Even if I don't feel like I deserve him, I want him. Filthy mouth or no. There is nothing in the whole of creation that could change how I feel about Ty. "I'm mad at you."

"Let's be mad at each other and then we can have make up sex."

"This isn't a joke, Ty," I say, shifting just a bit so that a shaft of moonlight from outside highlights his beautiful face.

"No," he admits. "It sure as shit ain't." He pauses. "So what do we do?" I glance away, and he leans in, pressing his cheek against my own. It feels extra wet now, like maybe he's crying, too, but I have no way of knowing how much of it is mine and how much is his, and I guess it doesn't fucking matter because we're both just a half, one wing on either side of a butterfly, unable to fly without the other.

"You promise never to call yourself a whore again." I sniffle a bit and sigh softly. "Only I'm allowed to call you that." I want to keep being mad. Why, I'm not sure. I guess I'm just not used to being happy. I wonder if I'll ever be. But it isn't possible to stay angry, isn't possible to drown in sorrow when there's a man that loves you pressing his face to yours, needing you as much as you need him. "And I don't care about what you did the past, not in the sense you think, so stop trying to clean yourself up for me. If I'd wanted a nice, clean boy, I'd have picked Noah Scott." I'm afraid this is going to piss Ty off, but he just chuckles. "And if you ever call yourself a cum dumpster again, I'll fucking cut off your balls. If anybody fits that description, it's me." Ty's muscles get stiff.

"Don't you even fucking dare," he growls, putting his hand

around my waist, pulling me to him. "You're the mother of my fucking children and the queen to the kingdom of my goddamn heart. I will defend you to the death, even against the enemy of your self-fucking-doubt."

"So you won't call?" I ask, hoping he can hear the fear in my voice. It might be an irrational fear, but it might not be. I don't want to test it. I really, really don't.

"I won't call," he says reluctantly. "But you have to promise to tell me next time you get scared of the baby. He's a part of you, too, Nev. Just like me. Don't be afraid of him."

"I'm more afraid *for* him," I say.

"Don't be," Ty says, kissing the tears from my cheeks. I reach up and grab his nose ring, using it to guide his face, focus his eyes on mine. "Your heart to heart chat didn't help?"

"It did," I say. "But I'm too broken to fix that easily. It's going to take a while."

"Let me help you."

"Why not the other way around?" I glare at him defiantly, sneak a cigarette out of his back pocket and put it between my lips. When my hand tries to steal his lighter next, he stops me.

"We'll get through it together. It's worked for us so far."

"Is this where you'd thought you'd be at the age of twenty-three?" I ask him randomly, just to see, just to delve a little deeper and see how he really feels. When he looks me square in the eyes and smiles, I know we're okay.

"I didn't even think I'd make it to twenty-three, so as far as I'm concerned, this is a success story." I don't hold back the next rush of tears that fall. Neither does Ty and his face looks stark raving beautiful with them decorating his cheeks.

"I heart the fuck out of you," I tell him simply. It seems like the only logical thing there is to say. He kisses me softly and pulls back.

"I heart the fuck out of you, too."

18

A few days after what Ty calls our *obligatory couple's brawl,*
I'm sorting through boxes in our bedroom, trying to make the
tight space work while simultaneously seeking out some of the
curiously odd Christmas decorations that Ty and I salvaged
from the New York house. Which, by the way, already has a
pending offer on it. Just in time for the fucking holidays.

I kick aside the box I was working on and move to the
next, looking for the reindeer with the cigarette in his mouth

and the snow man who's in the process of giving the middle finger. Ty says these unique treasures were passed down by his grandma, that no Christmas would be complete without them. So I keep searching, hoping I can find them before we start packing to head up to the cabin.

We're spending the whole week up there, us Regalis, along with our tagalongs McCabe and Scott. Should be exciting, especially since Zella will be there. God help me, but I want to play matchmaker between her and Noah. I sigh as I think about all the drama that will no doubt unfold within those log walls. It's going to be a real fuck fest.

I lean over the box and lick the tip of one of my fingers, dipping it into the bag of powdered sugar I stole from the kitchen. When Ty sees me eating this shit raw, he gets the chills and has to leave the room. Me, I could mix it with some water and drink the paste. Can't get enough of this shit. I watch my lick down with some strawberry smoothie from the nightstand.

"Find them?" Ty asks, moving into the room with Noah in his beautiful arms, wrapped tight in muscles and ink, the world's most beautiful sight. If I ever need a reminder that Ty belongs to me, that he's completely and wholly mine, all I have to do is see him holding our baby, and I *know*. Some primal instinct inside of me just won't shut the fuck up. *Ty McCabe is mine. That is our baby. I am the only woman who has the privilege of his seed.* It's a bunch of weird, prehistoric bullshit, but it's there and I accept it. I'll never tell Ty though, not unless he asks.

"Nope," I say as I watch him step over boxes and pause next to Noah's crib, pressing a metal studded kiss to his son's forehead before laying him down. "And it's pissing me the fuck off." I wipe a hand across my sweaty forehead. "Goddamn, I want a whiskey sour," I groan and Ty chuckles, nice and deep, low, suggestive. "Close the door," I command him when India moves past, brows raised and eyes averted. My sisters know not to bother us when we're in the bedroom.

"Your wish is my fucking command," he says, leaning over and shutting the door, turning the lock. He looks back at me with a sly smile.

"Unless you're made of bourbon, don't even bother to come over here right now. I'm operating with sugar not but no nicotine, no booze. Remember when I was pregnant with Noah?"

"Yeah, you were horny as shit," Ty says, and I roll my eyes, bending down and digging into the next box in line. *Aha. Found you, you stupid fucks.* I pull out one of my hip scarves that I've used to wrap up the fragile ornaments. It's not my taste – burnt orange and taupe, more my mother's style than my own, but I remember the day she got it for me. She went through these moods where she was the mother I thought I wanted, leading me on with false promises and smiles, only to watch me crash down even harder the next time she fucked up. *Fucking cruel ass bitch.* I pull the ornament out and see that it's neither of my favorites, but still nice – a big, fat ceramic dick hung from the balls with a blue ribbon.

"I miss your grandma, and I never even met her," I tell Ty. He grins and strips off his shirt, flashing me that perfect chest, his rock hard abs, the dark trail of hair leading into his pants. I try not to salivate and glance away, tossing the hip scarf onto the bed, so I can continue my search. The penis ornament gets thrown up along with it. Ty decides it's a cute idea to take it and hang it off our son's crib, so he can gaze at it with his fragile little being. "Thanks for scarring my baby for life," I tell him as he scoots over and falls onto the bed, looking up at me, black hair yellowed from the light on the nightstand. I have to really fight to keep my hormones in check, especially when he brings his ringed knuckles up to his stomach and runs them across the grooves of his belly like it's a fucking washboard.

"You actually remind me of her," he tells me, using his left hand to tug the hip scarf out from behind his head. The white fringe falls across his belly and already, I can feel my nipples hardening to points, my thighs moistening, my lips parting. I glance away.

"I remind you of your grandma? Do you know how fucked that sounds?"

"That you make me think of a strong, intelligent woman capable of changing the world by sheer force of will? Sounds pretty awesome to me."

"I love you," I blurt, and he grins. I stare at him staring back at me, and I fall more in love. Every time I think I've fallen too far, there's always somewhere else to go, and I know without a doubt that I am never getting out of this, would never want to get out of this, and am damned blessed for the opportunity to be here. "I'm glad you're not Rick," I say to which Ty gives me a really confused sort of look. But I don't know how to explain it to him, don't know how to tell him that he's exactly the sort of man I was looking for but the kind I was desperate to avoid. I don't know how to tell him that his corrupted soul saved my own, two negatives multiplying together to create a positive. So I just lean over and kiss him so hard neither of us can breathe, lock my lips to his so tight that by the time I pull away we're both gasping for air.

"I don't know who the fuck Rick is," Ty tells me. "But if I ever find out you kissed him like that, I'll have to search and destroy that son of a bitch." I stare at Ty for awhile and he stares right back, meeting the intensity in my gaze with some of his own, matching me at every turn, complimenting but not overpowering. We could've gone wrong together since we're so similar, could've exploded and ripped out one another's hearts, left them to bleed out in the hot, hot sun. But we didn't. We got it just right. Just fucking right.

"I want to dance for you," I blurt because as I'm standing there, fingering the fabric of a voluminous black skirt, I get a memory. Oh Noah Scott. I think of myself dancing for him, wanting to please him, loving him with my body. But I don't want my head filled with Noah Scott. All I care about, all I can think about, all I *want* to think about is Ty.

As soon as I say this, he gets really serious, sitting up and kicking off his boots before turning to face me. I can see sweat beading on his belly. Dancing has become this … thing between us. It has all of this meaning – the line he used on me when we first met, the stupid belly dancing video, the bar before we confronted Luis. Every time it gets brought up, something happens between us. And I want that for us, want our relationship to continue to change and grow, evolve so that it's always this passionate and fucked up and raunchy and sensual. I want to dream about his kisses every night and hold his hand every day. And I don't ever, ever want us to forget how good we've got it.

"Are you sure?" he asks me, and I know he's thinking about Noah Scott. But he shouldn't be. This isn't about Noah Scott. This is about him. Ty. Ty fucking McCabe, the man who stole my heart without meaning to, that crept into my life when it was at its darkest, lit up like the moon and showed me the way.

A light flush creeps into my cheeks which is so unlike me that I get pissed off.

"I'm going to have a fucking balloon for a belly soon enough, and I won't get another chance. It's now or Never," I tell Ty, crossing my arms over my breasts, wishing his hands were on them. He looks at me again, that tenderness filling his gaze, and I find myself paralyzed. The lust I can handle, but this … Goddamn it. He had to go there. He knows it screws with my head and he does it on purpose, bashing me over the head with that love until I get it, until I know I'm worth it. It'll be awhile, but I'll come around. I always do.

"I'd be honored if you'd dance for me, baby," he says and then his brown eyes start to sparkle, the love morphing into lust; desire creeping into the smirk on his lips. Even his dimples join along for the ride. "I was hoping you'd do this for me on our wedding night, but you know, there was the whole giving birth fiasco." I flip him off and grab a handful of items from the box. If I'm going to do this, I'm going to do it right. I'm going to dress up for him the way I did for Noah, but this time, when morning rolls around, I'll still be here beside him, always and forever. I bet we even end up in the same level of hell, buried side by side in matching fucking coffins. Or better yet, the same coffin, bones tangled up, scrambled into piles of who's who and whatnot. It's a morbid thought but somehow comforting at the same time. With Ty and me, it's not till death do us part. It's forever, just forever.

"I'm not promising I'll be any good though," I warn him before I step into the bathroom and escape my cocoon, transform into a butterfly, and get ready to show Ty my wings.

19

Deep breath, Never.

I touch the handle of the bathroom door, pausing for only a split second to check my appearance in the mirror. My dark hair, the mirror to my spirit, an inky well of blackness escaping my soul is coiffed atop my head, wrapped around with a purple scarf that hangs down, kisses the freckles on my shoulders. I've draped silver chains over the top, pinned bunches of silk flowers and crescent moons. I run my tongue over my lips, dyed a bright red, a pop of color in my pale face, like a strawberry, waiting to be plucked and kissed. My eyes are pulled and pinched back with the illusion of smoke, hazy and mesmerizing, truthfully deceptive, shaded just so, just enough to bring out the blue and green flecks in the hazel color without taking away from the stark beauty of the gray.

My belly, still flat but full with Ty's growing baby, has a butterfly pendant pierced through it, danging low, teasing the hem of my black skirt which hangs heavy off my hips, tied up with a fringe belt. The white tassels hang low and aren't afraid to move, blowing around as I turn, catching an imaginary breeze and taking off to the sound of silver bells, a string of which I've draped around my midsection and let hang down my side.

My left hand is a match for Ty's right, covered in twelve rings that I've borrowed from his grandma and my arms tinkle with bracelets. I smile wickedly at myself, biting my lip and letting my eyes trail down, across the deep line of cleavage, the turquoise top and the black half-vest that goes over it.

Ty is going to fucking flip.

I take another breath, close my eyes and imagine that the music I hear from the bedroom is taking me far away, to a different place, pulling Ty and I away from the world, so we can focus on each other and nothing else. He's the raven to my crow, and I couldn't imagine haunting this heavy world without him by my side.

I open the door and the thick, cloying smell of patchouli wraps around me.

"I found it in the dresser drawer," Ty tells me as I move forward, into the darkened room, lit up by two single candles on either side, framing the stage and the small area Ty's cleared of boxes for me. I know immediately when I fall into his line of sight, feel his eyes rake me and penetrate me, kiss and caress me.

I center myself as best I can and turn away from him, my eyes falling onto our sleeping baby, his soft face, his rosy cheeks. I lift my chin high and raise one hand over my head, palm up towards the ceiling, the other out at my side. And then I wait.

The room is so still, vibrating with electricity, even though I haven't moved, even though nothing's happened between us yet. The current song ends and the next begins. A deep hum buzzes through the speakers follow by the tabla. I let my lashes rest against my cheek and then I begin to move. I don't think about what I'm doing, I just do it.

My hips sway and my belly contracts, muscles sliding around, their memory better than my own. They know how to dance, and they're angry at me for denying them. Soon I'm spinning around and my hands are sweeping out before me, drawing back while my hips undulate in a slow circle.

I open my eyes and see Ty McCabe naked on our bed, legs crossed at the ankles, butterfly tattoos melting onto his shoulders. With the dim lighting and the flickering candles, I can almost imagine that they're alive, moving over his skin and inviting me over.

A breeze from the open window sneaks through and teases my heated flesh, draws goose bumps over my body. I imagine that it's Ty that's touching me with his calloused hands and his rings, holding me, possessing me.

I move for him.

My eyes close again, so I can reconnect with the music, feel the power of a hundred women, a thousand, a million, coursing through the earth, rising into the foundation of the house and finding its way to my bare feet. I feel powerful dancing there, my heart in my throat, my pulse wild. I feel real and organic and female. And I feel Ty's masculinity calling to me from across the room, from the bed where his hand's just dropped to his cock and he's stroking and pleasuring himself to thoughts of me and my heated warmth.

It's obvious to me then why I haven't danced for so long. To dance, to really show the world the sound of your soul through your body, you have to be whole. Where before, I was empty, I am now complete. Where before, I was barren, I am now full.

I open my eyes again and take a step closer, my skirt flowing free, teasing my calves, the bells on my waist jangling in tune with my bangles, with Ty's bracelets as he slides his hand up and down the length of his shaft, wishes for me with every part of his being. His moans join the drone of the music as I turn and my fingers move outwards, beckon him close. I tuck them against my chest and let my head fall back. Vaguely, I'm aware of my hair falling out of its bun, flowing free behind me as I spin in a tight circle so fast that I get dizzy.

"Come to me, baby," Ty says after awhile, voice husky, the sound colored with charcoal heat, like a fire long since left burning, still hot but not flaming. Now, it's sizzling. Now, although it isn't raging, it's at its hottest, its most sensual point.

But I don't go to him, not yet. I want to be possessed by him, but I'm also in control, and he knows that. The music asks me to show him with my hips what I'm feeling, so I dip the right side, then the left. I rise to my toes, and I tip my pelvis back and forth, sinking back down into a crouch and exploding out of it into yet another turn. I can't seem to stop making them, feeling that rush of blood to my head.

Ty starts forward, crawling across the bed, but I come to a sudden stop and lock my gaze on his, forcing him back against the pillows where he begins to beat at his cock with a ferocity that's almost frightening. A wicked smirk eats at my lips as a shimmy builds up from below, teases my body with small vibrations.

The song slows.

The tabla trails away.

I pause there in the pregnant silence, watching Ty, listening to him growling in his throat, waiting for me, wanting me.

Another song begins, slower this time, building momentum as it carries out the artists' wishes, twirling around the room and teasing the spirit the way good art always does. Whether it's a book, a painting, or a symphony, art is the dictation of the soul, the piece of beautiful blackness inside of all of us, and when it comes out, truly shows its face and breathes life into the beautiful air, there is nothing in this world that can compare.

"Babe, I need you," Ty says and this, this I can go to.

So I pad across the floor towards him, light as air, the vibrant, beautiful butterfly wings that are attached to my soul keeping me afloat.

Ty watches me hungrily, eyes sparkling dark, mouth twisted into an expression to match mine. We're just two little wickeds, me and him, just two nasty little wickeds.

I climb onto the bed and press my hands to his sweaty flesh, straddling him, pushing my bare cunt against his erection. His hand finds my hair, his lips my lips. He holds me in place while he kisses the fuck out of me. His tongue and mine dance to the music, pressing into each other hard, trying to blur that line between us, so that we're just one. Just one, fucking, twisted bit of soul in love.

Ty's other hand unhooks the vest in the front, unties the choli in the back. My tender breasts spill free and he drops his mouth to them hungrily, like he can't wait even a second longer or he'll explode. I wiggle into place and he helps guide me, dropping his hand from my hair to my hip, positioning me, so that my heat presses against his cock, invites him into soft wetness.

Ty enters me with a guttural groan, forcing me to grab his hair and hold him back. I'm afraid he's going to come too quick. I need him to wait for me, to feel every part of my body, taste every bit of my heart.

My slickness glides along him, teasing him, capturing him with that essential womanliness that is my fucking right, that bit of me that I betrayed by jumping from partner to partner. I abused her, stuffed her full but forgot to please her, and she's angry with me. Ty soothes this side of me.

While he kisses my breasts, bites my nipples, sucks them into his mouth, I spill words for him. I don't know what I say exactly, but I know I tell him I love him and his hands clamp tight on either side of my hips, guiding me, grinding me into him. When he pulls away from them, leaving them sore and wanting, he looks up into my face and breathes against my mouth, gazes at me with that careful tenderness I have to look away from. This time though, he grabs my chin and pulls me back.

"You deserve to be loved," he says which is so unexpected that I pause in our dancing rhythm. Our push and pull grinds to a halt with Ty buried inside of me, my skirt flowing around us like a flower. "You deserve it," he repeats. "And I'm going to be the man to prove that to you."

Ty pushes us over gently, falls against me and presses me into the bed with hot heat. My legs go around his back and cross at the ankles while he moves slowly, sweetly, carefully. Ty and I make a different kind of music that lasts long into the night, past the moment when the stereo goes quiet and into the early hours when the sun rises outside the window, kisses our bare flesh.

Like dancers in a choreography, we switch positions and taste each other, find solace in one another's flesh, keep the memory of our love alive and floating in the air like the incense that's long since burned out.

Ty spills himself inside of me again and again, and I drench him with my heat, and we mix saliva and sweat until we're just covered in each other, until the sheets are damp and the room is humid with the scent of our lovemaking. We go until we can't go anymore, until we fall to pieces together and glue ourselves back together in a tangled heap with his body still inside of mine, my hands around his neck, his forehead against my throat.

We stay that way until our baby calls out to us with a gurgle, brings us up and out of each other with a smile and a breath of fresh air that beckons in the new day.

20

The morning before we're supposed to load up and make the three hour drive to the cabin, Ty convinces me that I should tell my family about the baby. I'm not very far along in the pregnancy, so I don't know how great of an idea that is, but Ty seems pretty adamant about it. I wonder if it's because things are ... different now. That night, that dance, seems to have woven a spell around our family, and I don't feel so afraid of Noah anymore. I have a long way to go, sure, but I notice that I kiss his face more, hold him tighter, love him deeper. It's amazing how that works, isn't it? You think you can't love someone anymore because you love them an infinite amount of times more than you love your own soul, but then it happens. Miraculously, spontaneously, it happens and it's so fucking perfect that it makes you want to cry. I guess I shouldn't be surprised. Love is an all consuming thing, a well of infinite possibilities that stretches the limits of our own, individual universes and carries our spirits farther than we ever expected to go.

So, Ty wants me to tell my family about the new baby, okay. I'll do it. But I'm still Never Fontaine Regali-Ross-McCabe, and I'm a little bit of a bitch and ornery as fuck.

"What are you up to?" I ask him, eyes narrowed as he shifts his sweatshirt from one arm to the other. There's obviously something else wrapped up in there, and it's just a matter of time until I figure out what it is. "Is this about the doctor again?" Ty pauses and runs his tongue over his sexy lower lip. He won't stop on the whole doctor thing, but I haven't passed out again, and the spotting is minimal. I looked it up on my phone and it seems pretty common, so I'm not worried about it, but Ty is. It bothers him a lot, I think.

"No, but would you please reconsider going? This is really stressing me out, Nev, and remember, it's not just your body anymore – it's mine now, too." He tries to make this sound sexy, but there's this thread of fear woven into his words, this horrible nightmare of a thought that his love, his seed, his baby could somehow be responsible for something horrible, for threatening my life, for separating us when it should be bringing us together. I understand, but I still don't want to go.

"After Christmas?" I ask. He gives me a look and then sighs, nibbling at his lip ring and shaking his head. I've noticed that he's taken to wearing one of my bracelets at all times. My heart flutters in my chest, but I don't let him see it, maintaining my facade of stubborn unruliness. I can't let him know he makes me giddy and lightheaded or I'll never win another argument.

"You're so fucking stubborn," he says, but we both know that he is, too. Neither of us is going to get our way here, so compromises have to be made. The fact that we're coming to this conclusion together and without strife, is just further proof that we're meant to be. "If something happened to you, my soul would shatter." *How the fuck am I supposed to say no to that?* "But I guess there's no time, so ... you have to swear on my dick that you'll go as soon as we get back." I raise an eyebrow.

"Your dick?" Ty grins.

"I just picked the thing you love most in the world is all." I throw a pretzel at him and wish that it was a Marlboro. I'm kind of getting to the point where I wish and hope and pray that everything becomes a cigarette, just so I can stare at it and smell it. Addictions suck and mine is freshly revived, denied during Noah's pregnancy, rekindled in that brief period between, and laid dormant again. It's the worst fucking torture I've ever experienced. Fortunately, my other vice, my sexual addiction, gets to be fed full and often. Very, very often. *I'm going to end up with thirty fucking kids, aren't I? Aren't I?* When you're making constant, wild love to a fucking stallion like Ty McCabe, you sort of forget the basics. He's goddamn intoxicating, poisoning me with his presence, and I'm loving every damn minute of it.

"As fucking stupid as that is, fine. I swear on your big, hairy cock that I will go to the doctor after Christmas and have a strange man with latex gloves stick his hand up my vagina. Happy?" Ty grins and digs into his front pocket, pulling out a long, thin white piece of heaven, sliding it between his lips and lighting up with a merry jingle of bracelets.

India pops her head into the kitchen for a moment.

"First of all, you two are disgusting. Second of all, Beth says if she catches Never smoking, in the house especially, she's going to go ballistic." Ty laughs and scoots his way out the back door, abandoning me in my quest to 'quit'. At least for now. Once whoever this is comes out, I'll probably be right back at it again. I could ask Ty to stop with me for real, to give up smoking altogether, but I'm kind of living vicariously through the scent on his clothes and the ripe burst of flavor I get when I kiss his lips. Plus, I'm old school as fuck. Ty with a cigarette in his mouth turns me on. Sorry, antismoking ads. It probably shouldn't, but it does.

He only stays outside for a moment before coming back in and dropping his sweater to the table. As I'd suspected, there's something folded up underneath.

"Here," he tells me, smiling wickedly, pushing the black square of fabric towards me. "I got you a fucking present. I was going to wait until later to give it to you, but screw it. I want to see it on." I take the fabric in my hands and unfold it, finding myself face to face with the world's most fucking amazing T-shirt. My hormones try to get the better of me, filling my eyes with tears, but by sheer force of will, I push them back.

On the front of the shirt is a spinal cord and a ribcage with a tiny heart in the center, and down below, a baby skeleton curled up in the womb. It's so perfect, so Ty, so me. I clutch it to my chest.

"You know me too well," I whisper, voice so quiet it's almost impossible to hear. Ty steps forward and leans across the table, brushing my hair away from my forehead. He can hear me no matter how softly I speak or how loud I scream, and he will always be there. I know that now without a doubt. Somewhere deep, down inside of me, my heart continues to heal.

"No, I don't think so. I think we've got it just fucking right," he tells me, kissing me, promising me that all of these changes are good ones, that we're making the right decisions, that our life can only get better from this point forward. My phone rings and I glance at the screen.

"It's Zella," I say, slightly disappointed that the moment is over, but unable to hold back a smile when Ty presses his hot lips to my forehead. There will be more moments, more slices of tenderness and pleasure and passion. That's the beauty of being in love. I answer it. "You on your way?" I ask her, squeezing my shirt in my left hand, determined that after this call I'm going to go upstairs and slip it on. Ty watches me through half-lidded eyes and smiles.

I hear the worry in her breathing, know that something's wrong before she even speaks.

Just when you think everything else is under control, that you've got your shit together and your life in check, something else has to go wrong. Fortunately, it hasn't nothing to do with me this time.

"Never," Zella says, voice low and full of shame. "I think I'm in trouble."

TO BE

CONTINUED...

Never too Late #2: Never Let Go

Zella's Story

If you enjoyed this, you might like
Real Ugly (Hard Rock Roots, Book #1)

Excerpt Included!

CHAPTER 1

NAOMI KNOX

There's a metamorphosis happening right before my eyes. I'm watching a devil shed its skin, shrink its horns and grow wings. The dark haze in the air is lifting, banished by the bright lights of the stage. Even metaphorically, a trick like that is hard to pull off. I'm impressed. Or I would be if I didn't hate the asshole so much.

"He looks like a fucking angel," I whisper as I sip my beer.

"What?" Blair shouts, cupping her hand around my ear. I swipe some hair away from my face and lean over, so that she can hear me above the booming of the bass. It pounds down through the wood of the stage, into the concrete, and across the floor where it catches on the rubber soles of my boots and ricochets up through my bones. If I close my eyes, I can see it tainting my blood, forcing my heart to pump faster and faster, until I feel dizzy from the beautiful poison in the air. The phrase *slaying the crowd* wasn't made up off the top of someone's head; if the fucks on stage do it right, it really does feel like the music is killing you softly.

"Turner Campbell," I yell back at her, my lips brushing against the small, black plugs in her earlobes. "He looks like a fucking angel up there." Blair leans back and raises one pierced brow at me. Her blue eyes say that I'm full of shit. I take another sip of cool, cool amber and watch as she turns her heart shaped face to the stage. Her gaze rakes Turner from head to toe and then slides across the heaving, thumping crowd, landing right back on me.

"A fallen angel," she shouts. Pauses. "*Maybe.*"

I shrug and ignore her pointed stare, watching Turner as he moves across the stage, lights glistening off the blue-black highlights in his hair and making him look like he has a damn halo on his head. His brown eyes scan the crowd, catching on faces and holding them as he purrs into the microphone and caresses it like he fucking *owns* it. I bet every bitch in here can practically feel his hands on her body, taste his tongue in her mouth. *What am I shitting myself for? They've probably all had a nice, big slice of the real thing anyway.* Let's just say that Turner's reputation proceeds him.

Devil.

I have to remember that he's not just a devil, but *The Devil.*

I take another sip of beer and try to focus on something else – the crowd of people clusterfucking at the bar, the

mosh pit up front, Blair's white feather eyelashes. Nothing works. My gaze finds Turner Campbell again and stays there, focusing primarily on his lips and the words that tumble out of them.

"What the hell did you do to leave me broken, barren, and bleeding? What gave you the fucking right?" Turner sucks in a massive lungful of air, blowing his hot breath across the microphone and breaking my heart with a single gasp. I'm not alone. The crowd starts to hum, men and women alike pulsing with the heat and the energy of the song. *Goddamn, that's good,* I think as I allow myself to sink against the cool concrete of the back wall. *Doubt those lyrics are his though. Fucking hypocrite.* Just yesterday I walked in on Turner fucking a roadie over a PA speaker. When he saw me, he just pulled out and left the girl there with her panties around her ankles. She cried for a half a fucking hour. *Devil.* I want to hate him, but it's really hard from down here. I like it better when I'm backstage, when I can look at him hitting on groupies and roadies, watch him running his fingers across the lips of a dozen girls in a dozen cities. It's a lot easier to hate him that way. *How am I going to make it through six months of this?*

I finish my beer and push away from the wall, dropping the empty bottle on the edge of the bar before sneaking out a side door. My hands slide across a collage of torn stickers and scribbled Sharpie as I heave the heavy metal out of my way, snatching one last glance before I go at the lead singer of Indecency. Sweat slides down the tattoos on his neck and soaks into the fabric of his black T-shirt. Ironically, it's one of ours. *Amatory Riot.* I doubt he even really knows who we are. I bet one his roadie bitches dressed him this morning.

I drop the door shut behind me, not caring that the sound of it slamming is like a gunshot in the still air outside the Pound. I'm glad our set is over because it would be hard to follow an act like that. No matter what I think of Turner, his band is good. I guess they'd have to be since they're the headliners. Still …

I put a cigarette between my lips and light up. The tangy coastal air feels good against my moist skin and the breeze smells like salt, waking me from the buzzed trance I was nursing and thrusting me back into the real world. Not always a good thing.

"Hey, Naomi," a voice calls out from the end of the alley. I don't turn my head because there's only one person I've ever met that sounds like a demonic version of Mickey Mouse. "Hayden got drunk and vomited all over the bathroom. There's like three inches of fucking puke in there." Wren pauses next to me and tucks his skinny hands into the front pockets of his acid washed jeans. "It smells like tequila and it's making me sick." I take a drag on my cigarette and close my eyes. The music from inside is drifting through the walls and poking the bare skin on my arms like a chorus of needles. I sigh and flick my smoke to the grimy cement.

"So clean it up," I tell him as I crush the butt to ashes with the toe of my stiletto boot. "I'm tired of being Hayden's bitch." Wren watches me, but doesn't say

anything else. He knows I'll do it. That I'll walk in there and pick our lead singer up off the floor, wipe her down and strip her naked, put her to bed and tell her a goddamn fairy tale. I'm no stranger to cleaning up Hayden's messes. I just have to get my head in the right place before I do it. Wren shifts his weight to the side and continues to stare. "Fuck, don't just stand there and stare at me. You know I'll friggin' do it. Gimme a minute, why don't you?"

I turn away and start down the alley, back towards the front where bouncers in black shirts wait, passing around a silver flask and sharing a joint. They know me, so they don't say anything, just watch as I step into their circle and reach out my hand. Both items make their way to me quickly.

"I love your shit, Knox," says a man with bright blue eyes and a tattoo of a dragon curling up his left arm. I swig some of the alcohol from the flask. *Ugh. Cheap whiskey.* I wipe my hand across my mouth and hand it the person standing next to me.

"My shit?" I ask as I pinch the joint between my fingers and slide it into my mouth. I take a nice, long drag and wait for the smoke to fill my lungs and cloud my brain. I can't look at Hayden if I don't get fucked up first. Ever since that day, the sight of her makes me sick to my stomach. *God, I hate that bitch.*

"Your music. It's good shit." I blow white smoke into the air and smile with tight lips.

"If you ever call my music *shit* again," I say as I pass the joint to dragon-boy. "I will kick your fucking ass to the curb."

I make out with dragon-boy for awhile and stop just short of second base. He seems pretty pissed off, but I'm not a fucking whore, and I'm just not that into sex right now. My head feels light and fluffy, like it's been stuffed with cotton, and I'm having trouble walking. I have to stop in the alley and sit on the dirty cement, so I can take my stilettos off. It isn't easy to navigate in four inch heels, especially with the alcohol and the THC roiling around inside of me.

I throw the leather boots over my arm and stumble back to the bus, fully expecting to find Hayden right where Wren left her – drunk and drowning in puke. When I open the door, I get a whole other story.

"Right there, baby," Hayden is growling, hands curled around the edge of the countertop. Behind her, Turner Campbell is thrusting his dick like he's in a fucking marathon or something, gripping her skinny hips with white knuckles and squeezing his eyes shut tight. He doesn't even look up when I ascend the creaky steps.

"What the fuck, Hayden?" I ask, but she's so out of it that she doesn't hear me. Turner does, I can tell, but he doesn't respond either. Doesn't stop. The wet sound of their bodies sliding together makes my stomach twist

dangerously. Vomit climbs my throat, but I swallow it back. "Hey, motherfucker," I snarl, forgetting instantly about that angelic presence I saw on stage. It was all a trick of the light, a nice, fat slice of show business that he shoved down everybody's throat – including mine. He's back to being a devil again. How could I have ever forgotten? After what he did to me before, I should slit his freaking throat and toss him out the window, let the stray dogs in the alley finish him off. "Get off of her! She's fucking wasted, you asshole." I throw my boots on the floor and move forward, putting one hand on Turner's chest and shoving him back. He stumbles and hits the cabinets with a grunt, sliding to the floor with his dick hanging out of his pants and his shirt bunched up around his midsection. Bits of spiderweb peek out at me from under the black fabric of his tee, crawling down and wrapping his cock. He's even got tattoos on the damn thing. You'd think I'd have noticed that before, but I guess I was too busy getting my cherry popped to think about much else.

"What the hell?" he moans, putting a hand to his head and rubbing at his forehead with fingers wrapped in ink. When Turner pushes his hair back, the edges of star tattoos wink at me from his hairline. He's obviously trashed as shit, too, and doesn't make even a halfhearted attempt to stand up on his own. I roll my eyes and ignore him, throwing an arm around Hayden's waist as she tilts to the side and threatens to topple over. I don't have much love for the bitch, but if she dies, Amatory Riot is pretty much screwed sideways. It would be a sort of love/hate thing for me if she were to fall and crack her head open.

"Goddamn it, Lee," I growl at her as I drag her boney ass across the floor and kick open the doors to the sleeper section of the bus. Hayden is still covered in puke, so I force her to stumble into the shower and let her slump the floor. I turn the water on *cold*.

"Shit!" she shouts, her voice trailing off into a moan. Hayden's head slams into the tile wall and she starts to sob. "What are you doing to me?" she cries as I step back and run a hand through my hair. Blair is glancing at me from her position on the floor of the second bathroom, a sponge in one hand and a bucket in the other. Looks like most of the vomit is gone.

"Thanks," I say, but she's already shaking her head, tossing the sponge into the bucket and sitting up. The knees of her jeans are soaked through and her white tee is stained with something questionable. She looks pissed.

"Don't thank me, Naomi," she says as she stands up and leans against the door frame, popping a cig in her mouth as she relaxes against the wood. "This is Hayden's oversight, Hayden's tequila, Hayden's mess." Blair takes a drag and throws the cigarette into the bucket. "Stop taking responsibility for her shit." I don't respond because Blair doesn't know what happened between Hayden and me. If she did, she'd understand. I don't like her thinking I'm Hayden's lapdog, but what can I do about it? The bitch has shit on me for days. *God, I am so super fucked.* I shrug and turn around, ignoring the grunts of irritation from the bunk on my right.

"Fuck you, Wren," I snarl as I move past him and take

note of the other bunk. *Looks like Kash is in tonight. What a surprise.* Kash is having some kind of fucked up affair with two chicks – the driver for Indecency and the bassist from Terre Haute. He almost never spends the night on our bus.

I pause in the doorway and stare down at Turner Campbell and his flaccid dick.

"Get up, Turner," I bark at him, moving forward and poking his leg with my toes. "And get the fuck out. Go." He moans, but he doesn't move. I think he's even drooling on his shoulder. *Pathetic. If your groupies could only see you now.* "Turner. Get the hell off of my bus."

"What is your problem?" he whispers, sharp lips barely moving with the words. He sounds lucid enough, but he looks like shit. I put my hands on my hips and try to make a judgment call. It isn't easy with my head swimming like the Northern Pacific. I could go and grab one of Turner's band members, see if they'd come and get him, but I dread going on that bus in the middle of the night. That is, if their stupid ass bodyguard will even let me pass. Besides, the odds of finding anybody in that band that isn't trashed at this hour are pretty slim.

"Stand up," I command as I watch his hand travel between his legs, snap the empty condom off and toss it onto our carpet. My lips curl into a sneer, and I end up grabbing his arm and dragging him up off the floor. His skin is hot to the touch and sweaty as hell. *Please don't OD on my bus, you stupid fuck,* I think as I struggle to pull the world's biggest asshole to his feet. I don't like the man, by any means, but if he dies then I'm guessing they'll probably cancel the rest of the tour, and that would be a big ass, fucking drag for me and my band. Guess the least I can do is prevent him from drowning in his own vomit tonight. If keeping him on his back and wiping dribble from his chin will keep my dream afloat then the rest of the world be damned, I'll fucking do it. I can always take pictures as backup and sell them to the tabloids if everything goes to hell.

"Shit, Naomi," he growls, and I drop his arm like it's poisoned. Turner falls to his knees in front of me and leans against the wall, head hanging down between my legs and hands flat on the floor. "Just leave me alone. Leave me the fuck alone."

I stare down at the back of his neck, at the inky paw prints that climb his spine and disappear into his dark hair.

"What did you just say?"

Turner groans and lets himself slump fully against the cabinet before he opens his mouth and vomits right past that beautiful, little tongue ring of his. *What a friggin' douche,* I think, and then before I can stop it, my brain adds, *that remembers your name.* Hearing the three syllables of my earthly monicker pass through his lips was nothing short of a shot to the back of the head. I didn't even think that he knew the name of my band, let alone mine personally.

"Ah, shit," Blair says from behind me, making me jump as she sidles around me and stares down at the growing stain on the carpet. "This is great. Just great. Now we get to drive all the way to San Diego with the smell of Turner

Campbell's puke." She smiles at me with tight lips. "But hey, what's new, right? I feel like we're eternally in this fucker's shadow." She kicks Turner with the pointed toe of her red heel. "Still think he looks like an angel?"

I sigh.

"Just shut up, Blair, and help me pick him up."

She frowns at me and tucks some of her blonde and black hair behind an ear while I dig my arms under Turner's pits and try to drag him to his feet.

"And what, pray tell, are we going to do with him once we get him up?" she asks as she bends down and joins me, tits practically spilling out the top of the tight corset she's got on. All three of us groan as we shift Turner's comatose body between us, leaving his legs dangling on the ground like perverted puppet masters in the world's worst marionette show.

"Just put him in my bed," I say as I ignore another pointed stare from Blair.

"He's totally out, Mi. I doubt he could even get it up right now."

"Blair, seriously?" I ask her as we dump him on the bottom bunk and shove his legs up onto my black comforter. "I'm not even going to respond to that," I tell her as I hear a whimper from the bathroom and suddenly remember that I've left Hayden in an ice old shower. *Oops.* Blair and I exchange a look, and she sighs.

"Yes, I will clean up Campbell's puke as long as you don't start apologizing for him, too."

"Fuck him," I say.

"Good girl," she tells me and spins away on her heel while I retreat back to the bathroom and switch off the water. Hayden is curled into a fetal position, sobbing, and while that's not unusual, it's kind of disturbing to watch.

I grab a towel from under the sink and throw it to her. It hits her in the face and falls to the floor. Hayden lets out a wail that makes my teeth hurt, and I suddenly regret grabbing the bitch before she fell. *Should've let her crack her head wide open,* I think as I step forward and start to strip her down. She doesn't protest, just flops around limply and lets me tear off her expensive, designer clothing that's supposed to scream 'I'm a rebel!', but instead just makes her look like a fucking tool.

"Come on," I say to her as I grab her by the wrists. Don't need any help lifting this bitch. She weighs, like, maybe eighty freaking pounds. "You stupid, anorexic, motherfucker," I snort as I drag Hayden into the hallway and practically shove her onto the bunk opposite Turner. As soon as her wet head hits the pillow, she starts to snore. I watch her for a moment and turn away, catching a glimpse of Turner's shuttered eyelids and gently parted lips. Believe it or not, he looks like a fucking angel again. I flick one of his lip piercings with my fingernails and move back into the kitchen/living room area with a sigh. The pot and the whiskey have already abandoned me and left me alone with nothing but stark, white reality. "Is it wrong to hate someone so much it hurts?" I ask Blair as she sprays the rug with some sort of organic cleaner that I just know isn't going to work. The last one she used was made out of tropical

fruit and smelled like bubble gum; the piss stain on the hallway floor is still there. Enough said.

"Are you talking about Hayden or Turner?" Blair asks as we both look up and watch our driver/roadie/personal bitch, Spencer Harmon, step into the RV. She's got two armfuls of groceries and a wrinkled lip.

"God, what is that smell?" she asks as she sets the bags down and watches Blair go back to work, leather clad ass up in the air flashing a three inch line of butt crack. If I was into chicks, it'd be kind of hot.

"Turner Campbell's leftovers," I say as I pop in a cigarette and smoke it with short, sharp puffs like it's a cigar or some shit. I watch with disgust as goose bumps spring up all over Spencer's arms and legs. Her full lips part gently and her dark lashes flutter.

"Turner Campbell was here?" she whispers, and I can't hold back the scowl that crosses my face. I shouldn't get so annoyed at the girl. I mean, she's only one of thousands who've fallen for that man's charisma. *Myself included.*

"Yeah, and he's trashed as shit. I walked in on him and Hayden fucking."

"Hey," Blair snaps as she sits up and pushes her bucket away, wiping an arm across her forehead. "I had to watch the whole thing happen and even *listen* to it." I ignore her, and I don't ask why she didn't put a stop to it. Nobody stands up to Hayden except for me, and even then, it's questionable. Same thing goes for Turner Campbell, but not because he's scary like Hayden. He's just a god of the stage. He can do no wrong. I resist the urge to spit on the floor.

It's already bad enough down there.

"Oh," Spencer says, but the wonder in her brown eyes doesn't die and her skin prickles and crackles like it's been lit on fire. She removes the groceries like she's in a daze, pulling out healthy snacks like celery and carrots and broccoli that only she and Blair will eat. I can only hope there's something in there that's loaded up with carbs and sugar. "What time did he leave?"

"He didn't," I say, gesturing over my shoulder with my chin. I stab my cigarette out in an ashtray that's overflowing onto the table and shrug nonchalantly. "He's so fucked up that he couldn't stand. I put him in my bed." Spencer's eyes open wide, and I have to cut her off before she can even offer. "No, I'll sleep on the couch," I say and I can practically see her heart bursting out of her chest at the thought of spending the night within touching distance of Mr. Campbell. As irritating as the whole scene is, I'm glad because there is no way in shit that I would spend another night anywhere near that man. The first was bad enough. *Jesus, Naomi, that was six years ago. Get the fuck over it. You know he doesn't remember, so why should you?*

"Look at you," Blair says as she stands up, pulling the bucket along with her. "All empathetic and shit. Good for you, Naomi."

"Fuck you," I say as I give her the finger, grab a can of beer from the fridge and curl up on the black sofa that sits across from the door. I pop the top and nurse my drink while I watch Spencer finish putting away the groceries. When she's done, she just stands there and wrings her hands

like she's about to walk into an interview or something. "He doesn't bite," I say and immediately wish I hadn't. *Oh, wait. Yes, yes, he does.* I suck down half my can as I watch her watching me.

"You really do hate him, don't you?" she asks, and I shrug nonchalantly. But when I speak, I'm dead fucking serious. I raise my eyes to meet Spencer's.

"More than anyone else on this godforsaken earth."

About the Author

C.M. Stunich was raised under a cover of fog in the area known simply as Eureka, CA. A mysterious place, this strange, arboreal land nursed Caitlin's (yes, that's her name!) desire to write strange fiction novels about wicked monsters, magical trains, and Nemean Lions (Google it!). She currently enjoys drag queens, having too many cats, and tribal bellydance.

She can be reached at author@cmstunich.com, and loves to hear from her readers. Ms. Stunich also wrote this biography and has no idea why she decided to refer to herself in the third person.

Happy reading and carpe diem!

www.cmstunich.com